SACRIFICIAL LAMB CAKE

KATRINA MONROE

Sacrificial Lamb Cake
Copyright © 2014 by Katrina Monroe. All rights reserved.
First Print Edition: January 2015

ISBN-10: 1940215420
ISBN-13: 978-1-940215-42-6

Red Adept Publishing, LLC
104 Bugenfield Court
Garner, NC 27529
http://RedAdeptPublishing.com/

Cover and Formatting: Streetlight Graphics

To Aunty C, Lamb Cake's *first reader*

PART ONE

"And what does anyone know about traitors,
or why Judas did what he did?"

-Jean Rhys, *Wilde Sargasso Sea*

CHAPTER ONE

THE LAST TIME JUDAS ISCARIOT had found himself in the main hall of the Trinity Corporation, he'd been unceremoniously convicted of treason—a conviction that had earned him banishment to the white hell between planes of existence for all eternity. He shook his head. Never mind. This time would be different. The conviction had been almost two thousand years ago. Lifetimes past. Still, being in the same place, staring at the same polished marble, made him *itchy*.

Judas pulled a comb from his front pocket and ran it through his thinning black hair for the third time. His usual assurances and immaculate grooming wouldn't be enough for Trinity Corporation's board of directors. They knew him too well. His past. What he'd done. Hell, some of them had even witnessed it firsthand. Thinking about it, Judas shouldn't have accepted the invitation to present this idea, no matter how good it sounded. But the reward—how could he refuse something as tempting as redemption?

The conference room sparkled with readiness. Assorted doughnuts and pots of fresh coffee in three flavors—almond, vanilla, and coconut—covered a table along the wall. Rather than use the outdated white board, Judas called in a favor for something a little more high-tech. The collapsible projector screen framed by black velvet curtains took up the entire back wall.

He placed a clean, white packet at each board member's place at the main table before checking his watch. Five minutes to spare. Judas smiled.

At exactly nine thirty, the doors opened, and a bearded man built like a brick wall entered.

He met Judas's eyes and groaned. "You've got to be joking."

"It's good to see you too, Peter." Judas kept his hands firmly clasped in front of him.

"Does Joshua know about this?"

"I should hope so. He's the one who asked me to come."

Peter sat in the chair two places to the left of the head of the table and thumbed through the packet. "Yeah, well, this'd better be good."

Judas didn't have the chance to respond before the others trickled in and took their places. He recognized a few faces; others he could only guess—stand-ins to make him feel intimidated, maybe. Thomas and Matthew lingered over the coffee before sitting, shooting weary glances over their shoulders that Judas pretended to ignore. The last to enter were Joshua of Nazareth and the CEO, known inside the boardroom as G. They sat at the head of the table and looked up expectantly at Judas. Joshua waved and pointed to his hair, cut short and tight. He'd always had a thing about his hair. At least it was short now. Back in the day, it seemed Judas couldn't eat one meal without finding one of the Son's long hairs in his food.

G sat, wearing the grating expression Judas had grown to expect, as though there was something He wasn't telling. Which, of course, there was. "Well, well, Judas. My son tells me you have something to show me."

Judas nodded, rubbing his hands together, palms slick with sweat. "If you'll all open your packets to the first page, we'll get started." He waited until the rattling of pages settled. "I'm here because the Trinity Corporation and its affiliates, Christianity, Catholicism, et cetera are in need of an image clean-up. The public views Trinity as antiquated and irrelevant."

The board members shifted in their seats. Good. They *had* to know how much they needed him.

Judas continued. "The plan I've detailed in those packets is going to change all that."

"The Second Coming?" Peter tossed his packet to the middle of the table. "You call this a plan?"

Always the overachiever. Judas should have expected Peter to read ahead.

"Yes, but not in the way you're thinking."

"How exactly are we supposed to think of the Second Coming except in terms of the apocalypse?" Thomas batted a pen across the table between his hands. "That's, like, amateur dogma. Even the priests know it."

"This isn't what we talked about, Judas," Joshua said.

"How is the destruction of the Earth meant to improve Trinity's image?" Peter grumbled.

Fucking hell, they'd turned on him already. No matter. He'd dealt with worse. Roman soldiers leapt to mind. Judas retrieved the remote from his breast pocket and aimed it at the projector suspended from the ceiling. Lights dimmed, and an image of a woman appeared on the screen. The angle of the photograph made it look as though it had been taken from the street, aimed at an apartment window. Only her face was visible. Choppy, poorly dyed tangerine hair hung in her wide eyes. A tattoo of a small, black feather decorated the side of her neck, leading to a plaid poncho covering her shoulders.

When he turned to face his audience, Judas was met with sneers. "Page four details everything you need to know about her. She is to be the new face of the Trinity Corporation."

Thomas raised an eyebrow. "She's a hippie."

"Joshua is a hippie." Judas nodded in his direction.

"It's true," Joshua agreed.

"Oh, give me a break." Peter rubbed the bridge of his nose. "You can't be serious. This woman... she's pathetic."

"So were you, once upon a time," Matthew said.

"She's a lesbian, for God's sake." Thomas threw up his hands.

G cleared his throat. Thomas muttered an apology.

Judas put up his hand and waited for quiet. "Yes, yes, she is all those things, but that's why she's perfect." He pressed another button on the remote, and the woman's image was replaced with a graph. "This is your demographic. The world isn't the same as it was when you all lived. The harder you fight against the current of change, the quicker you'll drown." Judas clicked back to the woman. "She has the potential to reach people who otherwise would turn a blind eye to your message. That's all she'll be: a messenger."

"A messenger?" Thomas asked. "We did that. Remember Joan of Arc? That was a disaster."

"A figurehead then. All of the representation with none of the actual power."

"Like the Queen of England," Joshua said.

"Like Joshua." Thomas snickered.

"Oh, *real* funny, Thomas."

Judas rolled his eyes. Two millennia and the trauma of death hadn't changed a thing. They still bickered like children.

"Sorry, Joshua, but it's not going to work. Judas is blowing smoke up your ass. Again." Red bloomed in Thomas's cheeks.

Judas stiffened.

"Figurehead or not, should these events you've outlined take place, there could be severe consequences." Thomas scooted forward in his chair. "What happens when the guys with the fire see this woman acting like she's the Second Coming and proceed with their end of the deal? Gabriel told me the watchers have had their hands full trying to keep tabs on the increasing number of scouts, which, I might add, is a fucking chore in and of itself."

"They won't." Judas struggled to keep his tone calm. "The Grigori are prone to exaggeration. Who really takes them seriously, anyway?"

"Look who's talking," Peter said.

"I wonder then. Who put you on to this woman in the first place, Judas, if not a watcher?" G eyed Judas over his glasses.

Judas reddened.

Thomas leaned forward over the table. "You could inadvertently put the wheels of the apocalypse into motion, and then we'd have a real mess on our hands."

"It won't."

"But how do you know—"

G smacked His hand on the table. Silence fell over the room. "I've heard enough arguing for one afternoon. If you knew the half of what constantly bounces around in my head. The whining alone... Anyway, Judas has a point. We're losing them. The message I gave to Joshua to carry into the world has been twisted beyond recognition thanks to time and tongue. This woman is perfect."

A surge of grumbles washed over the room while Judas breathed a sigh of relief. One step closer to freedom.

G continued. "Okay, then. That only leaves the matter of an escort, someone to implement the points in Judas's plan on behalf of Trinity."

"I think Thomas would be an excellent choice, sir," Judas said.

Thomas glared.

G smiled. Judas saw that mischievous look again. "I disagree."

Judas's fists clenched. "Dare I ask...?"

"As a matter of fact, I'm glad you did." G waved his hand dismissively. "The rest of you can leave. Judas and I have something to discuss in private."

Judas felt sick. It was happening all over again. He wanted to run but couldn't. Where would he go, anyway? Back to the pit? No, thank you. *Idiot.* This had been His plan all along. How could Judas have been so stupid as to think G would actually *solicit* and then *accept* advice from him? Judas had gone soft in his afterlife.

Thomas shot him a wicked grin before exiting the conference room behind the others. Only Joshua looked at him with any sympathy, though Judas wasn't positive it was genuine. Joshua'd probably been part of it. *Never let it be said the Son didn't believe in an eye for an eye.*

Once the room was cleared, G gestured to a seat beside him. Mentally bracing himself, Judas sat, keeping his gaze focused on the area between G's eyes. He couldn't bring himself to look directly into them, but Judas knew better than to look completely away.

"You look good, Judas."

Judas stretched his lips over his teeth in a kind of smile.

"The last time I saw you, your face was a much more dramatic shade of purple, wasn't it? Eyes rolled back in your head, rope burns around your neck. Gruesome."

Judas shifted uncomfortably. His death had been long and excruciating. It would have been longer had G not intervened.

G folded his arms over his chest. "We find ourselves in a fortuitous situation, Judas. I believe what we have here is an opportunity."

"Nothing is fortuitous with you. Planned or connived, maybe."

G raised an eyebrow. "Don't be coy with me. You owe a debt, and it seems I am in need of some assistance."

Judas's voice rose. "Then why bother with this whole bullshit charade? Putting me up in front of the men like that! *And* Joshua... You forced me to face their contempt after I'd already been punished."

Two thousand years in that white room. Waiting. Feeling every torturous second.

The door opened, and one of the Archangels, Gabriel, peered inside, illuminated by his sword, which shone so brightly it appeared to be on fire. "I heard yelling. Everything okay?"

Judas breathed deeply. It'd been a while since he'd felt such intense loathing. It cleared his head a little.

"Everything's fine, Gabriel. Thank you."

The angel nodded and closed the door behind him.

G turned to Judas, His eyes narrowing. "I don't have to justify my actions to anyone. Least of all you."

Teeth clenched, Judas stared directly into those burning blue eyes. In them he saw the futility of arguing further. He couldn't win this fight. But somehow, simply giving in again after all he'd been through felt like more of a loss than anything *He* could do to him. "Why me?"

G smiled. "Because it has to be you."

Judas remembered the reward he'd been promised in exchange for the presentation. "What's in it for me, if I go along with this insanity?"

G touched his nose. "Besides settling your debt? I haven't quite decided. Though, I think you'll agree *not* going along with it would be exponentially worse."

Debatable, Judas thought.

"Shall we begin?"

Reluctantly, Judas nodded.

G gripped Judas's hand tightly enough to break it. "I'm trusting you with my plan. Don't fuck it up."

A wave of invading thoughts flooded Judas's mind, images and sounds he'd never seen or heard before with G's voice over it all, directing his mind, guiding him. All that was to happen, had happened, and could possibly happen should things deviate from the plan.

"Free will," G said. "It's a bitch."

Aches wracked Judas's head. It felt as if the sound of G's voice would bleed out of his ears. Just when he thought his brain would explode, a shock pierced his hand and traveled up his chest, hitting his heart like a punch.

"Clear." G laughed.

Another jolt came, more painful than the first. Breath filled his lungs, and his vision fogged. Judas fell backward, the girl's image the last thing he saw.

The Archangel Gabriel held his flaming sword aloft to better admire the blue-green flames licking the steel. After the war, he'd been one of the few loyal to the Father and had been granted not only a gift but a sacred duty.

He straightened his breastplate, polished to a blinding gleam, and continued pacing the hall outside of the main conference room where G sat with the traitor. Gabriel shuddered. Thinking about the traitor sent waves of disgust through his body. In his opinion, the traitor should never have been allowed to desecrate the halls Gabriel was charged with protecting. It was an invitation for trouble.

Gabriel passed the doors and heard a crash. It had to be the traitor. Even he wouldn't dare lay a finger on G. Honestly, Gabriel would rather have ignored the traitor's cries of pain. Such was the life of an angel, however. Goodness won out once again, and Gabriel entered the room.

G sat alone at the head of the table, smiling.

Gabriel cleared his throat. An affectation—angels didn't produce phlegm. "I heard..." He hesitated as his gaze fell on a tipped chair. "A bang."

"A bang?"

Gabriel nodded.

"Ah, well, as you can see, everything is fine here."

"Right. Well, back to my post then."

"Actually." G stood. "Now that you're here, I need to ask a favor."

A personal favor for the Alpha and Omega? The honor was more than Gabriel could have ever dreamed of. *Won't Michael be jealous when he hears?*

"Anything, sir." Gabriel genuflected.

"I'll be needing that sword back."

He whimpered. *Anything but that.*

CHAPTER TWO

HER NAME WAS RAINFALL ON the Desert Plains Johnson. Unless someone desired pain like a thousand wolves gnawing on their innards, they called her Rain.

This morning, a ray of direct sunlight scalding her pupils through her eyelids was Rain's alarm. She opened her eyes. A six foot tall sculpture made of dismembered plastic dolls and cattle skulls painted a shade of green that could only be described as *baby shit* greeted her. Bits of paint had dripped from the statue, speckling the carpet. To any outsider, it would look as though the sculpture belonged in the room. Half-finished canvases and sketches were strewn about as if a museum of amateur art had exploded. Rain hadn't finished a piece of art since leaving school. The sculptures, though—an upright cat with a disembodied head, a vagina made of welded cutlery, and now this thing—all belonged to Francine.

"Do I even want to know?" Rain asked.

"Oh, good, you're up," a sprightly voice said from the floor beside the bed. A fountain of red curls shuddered and danced. "I was beginning to think I would have to resort to desperate measures."

"Such as?"

Francine chuckled.

"What time is it?" Assigned to work the dinner shift, Rain refused to leave her bed until the last possible minute.

"Two."

Rain kicked the tattered quilt from her legs and stretched, feeling the last of her early twenties leave her body with each pop of her joints. It wasn't until she swiped her legs over the sheet that she discovered she wasn't wearing pants.

She looked down then brought her eyes up to Francine. "Why aren't I wearing pants?"

"You really ought to put a fan in here or something. You were sweating."

The room wasn't warm. Rain had been having nightmares again.

"Or you could sleep in your own room," Rain said, anxious to keep the subject away from her fear of the dark.

Francine emerged from the side of the bed, wearing only a paint-splattered T-shirt and boxers. She sat next to Rain's feet and smiled. "I was already here."

Boundaries weren't something Francine confined herself to. *Personal space* was just as foreign a concept. Usually, Rain brushed it off as a byproduct of being raised in Europe—Francine had never told her where specifically—but she drew the line at unconscious stripping whether they were in one of their sleeping together phases or not.

"Give me my pants."

Francine pouted, but she retrieved the sweatpants from a rumpled heap of clothes next to the door.

Wriggling into them, Rain fell back against the pillows. She still wasn't quite ready to leave her bed, but at least she wasn't half-naked. *Progress.* She pointed to the baby-shit-colored sculpture. "When did this happen?"

"I couldn't sleep. Do you like it?" Francine smiled expectantly.

"What is it?"

"A comment on the futility of young motherhood."

Rain nodded, which, given her close proximity to heavy objects, was the safest reaction to the piece: thoughtful and approving. But really, she had no idea what the hell Francine was talking about. It'd been this way between them since art school. While Rain had focused on learning to master fabric folds and realistic faces in paint, Francine focused on making statements—the more vague and obtuse, the better. Each would show the other her work and be met with a nod and a smile.

"I'm still working on it." Francine stared wistfully up at her work. "Needs another layer of paint. Maybe a few more limbs." She pointed to the alarm clock, half buried under a pillow on the floor. "We should probably go to work."

Groaning, Rain rolled to the side of the bed and let her legs fall to the ground before marionetting herself into a standing position, her strings pulled by some invisible force that some might've called the spark of motivation. If she was going to be of use to anyone, she'd need coffee, but the kitchen was so far away...

"I'll turn the pot on. You get in the shower."

Some days, Rain loved the girl.

Opening his eyes was a mistake. Sand fell into them. His nose. His mouth. Every orifice was pelted with the stuff, adding to the mound covering his chest and stomach. Judas lifted his arms, flinching at the pain, and felt wood. It smelled of dirt and age. Lying in a wooden box. The bastard had woken him in his coffin.

"Motherfucker."

Language, Judas.

Judas tried his best to breathe. Not having done so in more than two millennia, his lungs (how did he have lungs now?) weren't ready to accept the burden of rapidly thinning air. "How do you expect me to do anything trapped in here?"

I don't.

Judas waited for more of a response, but he was met with silence. If G was to be a constant companion in his thoughts, Judas thought he'd rather be back in his prison.

His elbows scraped the sides as he struggled to move in such a cramped space. How the hell was he supposed to get out? Something sharp pricked the soft part of his inner thigh. Grunting, he reached down and pulled the object toward his face. There was no light, so he couldn't exactly see it, but as he ran his fingertips over the wooden shaft and sharpened blade, Judas realized it was a shovel.

Dig.

It was a miracle Judas didn't drown in the sand as he dug his way to the surface. *Ha, miracle.* He tried to remember a time when that word had evoked a sense of wonder in him. It'd been years. Millennia. Back before he'd met the man who claimed to be the Messiah and followed him blindly into the desert to starve and pray. What a *putz* he'd been.

Sure, the man turned out to be The One, but it didn't mean Judas couldn't harbor a little resentment. *Any sane man would.* Resentment, though, was a far cry from treachery. Judas had been a loyal man: to his brothers, to his God. But, if he'd have known what an asshole his God was before accepting the role of disciple to the Messiah, he would have jumped on a horse and ridden to India or China. He'd heard their gods were kind. No floods or mass killings for those guys, no sir. At least, that'd been the rumor. Yet, here he was again—déjà vu in the worst of ways.

Hindsight was always twenty-twenty.

Judas broke through the surface just as the sun was setting. The heat, however, hadn't let up. The desert. Again. If he remembered correctly, there would be a city a few miles west of where he was buried. He wasn't anxious to see how much it'd changed in the millennia since his death, but he didn't stand a chance against the snakes and buzzards.

Looking down in the slowly fading twilight, Judas discovered, instead of the tatters he expected, he wore a suit much like the one he'd worn in the Trinity conference room. At least he wouldn't have to explain his appearance.

You're welcome.

Judas rolled his eyes.

You know where to go. Get there by tomorrow.

"And exactly how do I do that with nothing but the clothes on my back?"

A light flickered in the hole he'd just dug himself out of. Upon closer inspection, Judas discovered a duffel bag tucked into the corner of the mutilated coffin. The final rays of sunlight glinted off the zipper. He was sure it hadn't been there before.

"What's in there?"

No answer. Of course not. Why would He?

Not wanting to jump back into the hole, Judas attempted to catch the straps with the handle of the shovel. It barely reached halfway into the hole. *Son of a bitch.*

"You couldn't have put it up here? Fucking Christ." He instinctively flinched. "Get a grip," he muttered.

Using the shovel as support, Judas lowered himself into the hole to retrieve the bag. It was heavy and awkward to lift, so he threaded his arms through the straps, carrying it like a backpack, and struggled to pull himself plus the added weight to the surface.

He panted heavily. This had to be too much activity for the newly alive. How much could his two-thousand-year-old body take? Judas punched the bag into something mildly softer and lay down, resting his head on it. Forget the city. Maybe he'd just sleep here. It was quiet, and it'd been a long time since he'd been able to see the stars from below.

A soft breeze blew over him, and his nose twitched. Something smelled like death. He groaned. It was him.

Being a waitress at the Maxwell Street Bar was tolerable on nights when the dining room was packed and Rain made enough in tips to cover at least one of her steadily expanding pile of bills. On nights like tonight though, when she took to cleaning the booths in Francine's section to stave off the boredom, she wondered why she hadn't given more thought to her life choices.

Tonight, the management had implemented a new "Kids Eat Free" night, demoting the restaurant from *decent* to *hell-no-I-don't-want-to-go-there*. Rain dreaded having to put up with children, so the move had ruined her night before it'd even begun.

It wasn't that she hated kids. Hate was a strong word reserved for public restrooms and local news anchors. She just had trouble seeing them as people. Children called to mind the troll that lived under the bridge in *Three Billy Goats Gruff*.

"It'll be fine," Francine had said when Rain's third table of children was seated.

And it was, until some little brat demanded to "devour the unborn."

"Eggs," his exasperated mother clarified. "He wants eggs."

Rather than risk another tantrum like the one at her first table—
but Mooooooooom, I want the dinosaur macaroni—Rain simply nodded,
went back to the kitchen, and bribed the cook with a flash of her bra
strap to make them.

Eight o'clock came and went, trolls were sent back beneath their
bridges, and she had no choice but to do side work.

Hours passed.

With nothing else to clean, Rain wandered back into the kitchen
and leaned against the salad dressing station, dunking stale croutons
in low-fat ranch until the end of her shift.

All things considered, Maxwell's wasn't the worst place to work.
They let her wear jeans and didn't care if she snacked in the down
time. Joey, the night manager, didn't harass her if she occasionally
showed up late, hungover, or both.

But Rain's parents (a couple with unfairly usual names, Emily and
Daniel) had instilled in her a special kind of guilt—guilt for being a
human on Earth—that chipped away at her laid-back approach to life
when she allowed herself the time to think about it. According to them,
Rain and her siblings, River and Sycamore, and every other human
being for that matter, had a duty to Mother Earth to live in constant
awe and humility of her offerings and to cast off all contemporary
conveniences. Basically, in the eyes of Mr. and Mrs. Johnson, if you
didn't shit in a hole in the ground and drink directly from the udder
of a cow, you were single-handedly destroying the planet. Serving
fatty hamburgers to the public, her gratitude for indoor plumbing,
and her closet full of polyester T-shirts guaranteed Rain the position
of family black sheep. She hadn't spoken to them in years.

Not all her parents' influences fell to the wayside, however.
Though she obediently carried the charred, plated carcasses of various
domestic animals, Rain couldn't bring herself to actually eat one. The
last time she'd eaten any flesh was when Francine tricked her into
eating a slice of "vegetarian" bacon. As much as Rain hated to admit
it, it had been delicious, and now she could not stop herself from
salivating at the thought of it.

Rain had worked her way through half the tin of croutons when Joey came to the kitchen to tell her she had a table.

"Can't Francine or Margo take it? Tonight's been shit, and I've only got twenty minutes left."

Joey squinted and looked up at the ceiling, his tic when attempting to avoid confrontation. He was a big guy, and the gesture felt strange coming from someone who moonlighted as a bouncer. "I already cut Francine, and Margo just took a table. Last one, I promise. Then you can go, okay?"

Rain stuffed a soggy crouton in her mouth and nodded. She needed the money, but the last table of the night was always the most difficult to handle and left the worst tip. She left the kitchen and, eyeing the customer from a safe distance, concluded that tonight would be no different.

A frighteningly pale man in a black suit sat alone at the edge of the booth with one leg protruding from beneath the table as though he were waiting for an excuse to run away. His near-black hair was slicked back, exposing a large forehead. He checked his watch every few seconds until he saw Rain walking in his direction. His leg disappeared beneath the table, and he sat up a little straighter, never taking his eyes off of her. The man looked like Dracula's accountant waiting for his nightly goblet of A-positive. Weren't today's vampires supposed to be sexy and vegan?

Rain approached, keeping her distance. She turned her side to him and aimed for the door just in case she needed to run for it. The acrid stench of rot emanated from the man, and she struggled not to gag.

"Welcome to Maxwell's." She slipped into the usual script to make the interaction as quick as possible. "My name is Rain. Can I get you something to drink?"

The man seemed to consider her question for a long time. Finally, he nodded. "Water, please."

Margo had once drawn up a formula to estimate the average tab of a customer based on the brand of clothing he or she wore. Rain couldn't keep up with the details, but the gist of it was: the smarter the suit, the cheaper the chump.

"Water, sure thing." Her glance flickered to the menu, untouched at the opposite end of the table. "Would you like a minute to look at the menu?"

Again, he considered her question, this time with his ear inclined upward as though he were listening, before answering, "Actually, Rain, forget the water. I'd like to talk to you about our Lord and Savior, Jesus Christ."

Sweet hell, he was one of *them*. It was as though they sniffed her out. In the last month alone, she'd been hounded no less than twelve times by their black-tie-clad missionaries. Joey could fire her if he wanted to, but she wasn't in the mood to humor this guy, especially without a substantial tab and a twenty-percent tip.

"Look, guy, we're closing up soon. If you want food, I'll take your order and wait patiently behind that kiosk while you scarf it down. If you want to preach, go somewhere else."

His eyes narrowed, and he stood, clearing Rain's height by a good foot and a half. He reached out a bony hand and grabbed her.

Struggling to yank her arm from the man's grip, she yelled for Joey.

The kitchen doors burst open, and Joey barreled through like a linebacker. The pale man let go as soon as Joey was within arm's reach.

"You need to keep your hands off my servers, sir," Joey said.

"It was a misunderstanding." The pale man looked pointedly at Rain.

She shuddered. This was the kind of shit her mother warned her about.

"Even so, I think it'd be best if you were on your way." Joey took a step forward. The pale man stood his ground.

"Fine." He shot Rain one last piercing look and then headed for the door.

Joey waited until the pale man was gone before sighing. "Want to tell me what that was about?"

"Jesus freak."

Joey nodded. "Guy didn't seem that tough. I thought lesbians could fight."

She punched his arm.

"Point taken."

"Can I go home now?"

"Yeah, go ahead. Let Margo walk you out, though. Jesus Freak might be lurking in the parking lot."

"Way to make me feel better, Joey."

He patted her shoulder and ambled back toward the kitchen.

Margo finished up with her last table while Rain counted her tips. Forty-seven dollars and eleven cents were all she had to show for seven hours on her feet. If she planned to pay her half of the rent this month, she'd need to make at least three hundred dollars over the next two shifts, one of which was a weekday lunch. Rain leaned her head back against the wood paneling and groaned.

"That bad, eh?" Margo stood in front of Rain with her apron slung over her shoulder, barely concealing the fifty-something-year-old cleavage struggling to escape her shirt.

"I need another job."

"I hear ya, sweetie. Barely reached my usual hundred tonight." Fifty-something-year-old tits were still tits, and they worked for Margo. She flirted, cajoled, and pitied her way into men's wallets. The rumor was she used to be a stripper, but they'd retired her over an issue of cellulite.

Rain could never have been a stripper. She was awkward with women and uncomfortable with men who expected a guilt-free flirt along with their burger special. Mostly, she just made sure they had all the ketchup they needed and sent *tip me* vibes while they filled out their credit card slips. Obviously, she needed a new strategy. Or a new job.

Fuck it. A new *life*.

"Ready to go?"

Margo pulled the chopsticks from her hair and let it fall in a box-blonde cascade down her back. "Always."

Outside, the parking lot was empty, save for Margo's bright red Miata, Joey's truck, Rain's piece of shit Toyota, and a pair of cars abandoned by patrons who had either been too drunk to drive or had caught a ride to someplace better. Margo set off for her car while Rain crept towards the Toyota, looking underneath to make sure the pale man hadn't decided to surprise her. She glanced in the backseat and, satisfied that he wasn't waiting for her inside the car, turned to Margo and waved.

After a battle with the rusted door handle, Rain climbed inside, stuffed her apron in the back seat—one of these days she'd remember to bring it in to wash—and turned the key in the ignition. She looked out the driver's side window, and her breath caught. The pale man stood close enough to kiss the glass, his face ghost-like in the sparse street lighting. Fear coursed through her. She fumbled with the lock. *Shit, shit, shit.* Stupid thing always jammed at the worst times.

The pale man reached into his jacket pocket. Rain braced herself for the worst. *This is how I die.*

But when the pale man removed his hand, he held an envelope: black, small, and with a gold seal affixed to the back. He tapped twice on the window.

"Fuck off." Rain praised herself for not letting her voice shake.

His hand balled into a fist, and Rain thought he was going to punch through the glass. He looked as though he could. She fumbled for the shifter. Putting his hands up, the pale man mouthed, *Wait.*

Rain held her breath. With slow movements, he lifted her windshield wiper, placed the envelope beneath it, then took several steps backward until he was barely visible in the darkness. Rain jerkily wrenched the car into gear and raced out of the parking lot.

CHAPTER THREE

ESPITE SEVERAL ATTEMPTS TO GET rid of it on the way home—flicking her windshield wipers and driving more erratically than usual—when Rain pulled into her parking space, there the envelope sat, almost stubbornly, beneath the wiper. It was ridiculous to be afraid of it, but she felt trapped in her car, as if the envelope would explode the moment she opened the door. Sleeping out there until Francine came out to collect her wasn't an option. To describe the neighborhood as sketchy would be generous, and though the calendar insisted spring had sprung, Minnesota didn't give a shit. It would dip well into the twenties overnight.

This is stupid. It's probably just an invitation to their next exorcism or virgin sacrifice.

Still, it took an extra few seconds for Rain to work up the nerve to finally get out of the car. She slammed the door behind her and grabbed the unnerving envelope before running through the security door and up the stairs to her apartment.

Inside, Francine reclined on the futon, wrapped in a crimson kimono, her feet resting in a mop bucket full of water. Blue and pink opalescent beads floated at the top. An obscenely high-pitched voice warbled from the radio in the corner. Rain ignored the opportunity for comment and made a beeline for the refrigerator where she found an unopened box of white wine. *Thank Christ.* She paused, stricken at the expression. *Shake it off. Lubricate with alcohol. Repeat.* After tossing the envelope on the counter, she filled a plastic cup to the brim, sipped the overflow, and then sank cross-legged on the carpet next to the futon.

Francine patted her head. "Rough night, cupcake?"

"Think you could turn the radio down? And you're sloshing water on the carpet."

"So that'd be a 'yes.'"

Rain swallowed a large gulp of the wine. It tasted like piss, but it'd get the job done.

"Come on. Tell mama." Francine pulled her wet feet from the bucket, planting them in Rain's lap.

Rain drained the cup before diving into the events of the night, starting with the croutons (which were unusually stale) and ending with the pale man planting the envelope.

"Is that what you threw in the kitchen?"

Rain nodded.

"What's in it?"

"How should I know?"

Francine gasped. "You didn't look?"

"You didn't see him, Francy. This guy was fucking weird. Like a vampire trapped in a day job. I was happy to get away from him without a bullet in my face."

"Jesus, Rain, it's an envelope." Francine hopped from the futon and strode into the kitchen. She snatched it off the counter and held it up. "Do you think he's going to jump out of it once you lift the flap?"

"No. But there could be, like, anthrax or something in it."

Francine laughed. "Anthrax? Did you take a job as a senator and forget to tell me?"

Rain shrugged. Francine really didn't get it. Rain knew it sounded silly, but some primal, instinctual fear had risen from her bowels each time the pale man had looked at her. Okay, so there probably wasn't anthrax in the envelope, but whatever *was* in it couldn't be good.

"It's cash." Francine's voice was giddy.

"What?" Rain stood and rushed into the kitchen.

"At least a grand here. And a note."

Folded once, the paper was soft but sturdy, like the bills it encased.

Francine handed it to Rain without looking inside. After a moment's hesitation, Rain unfolded the note:

Dear Rainfall on the Desert Plains Johnson,

Your presence is required at the Dunkin' Donuts location on the corner of 5th Street and 2nd Avenue in Minneapolis at ten a.m. tomorrow. The enclosed money is a good faith payment for services to be requested at this meeting. Please do not bring friends as the information I wish to divulge is of a confidential nature. I assure you this is a legitimate business offer.

Regards,

Jude I., Trinity Corporation

"Services? What the hell does that mean?" *And how does he know my full name?*

Francine snatched the note from her and skimmed it. She snorted. "Does he know you're a lesbian?"

Rain poured another cup of the piss wine. "Well, it doesn't matter because I'm not going."

"What do you mean you're not going?"

"I'm not an idiot. This guy could be a psychopath."

"A loaded psychopath." Francine fanned her face with the bills.

Rain raised an eyebrow.

"Look, what's the worst that could happen? He's asking to meet you in a public place during a time when there's sure to be at least a few people around. Go, hear what he has to say, and make sure he leaves first so he can't follow you."

Rain looked at Francine over the rim of the cup. "You sound like you've done this before."

"I watch a lot of gangster films."

Rain's stomach dropped. The mob? Jesus, what would they want with her? She wasn't even Italian. "I don't know..."

Francine rolled the bills and stuffed them up Rain's shirt into her bra. Loosening the delicate ties, Francine let her kimono fall open. "Tell you what: I'll go with you, but I'll wait outside so you're not breaking the 'no friends' rule." She wrapped her arms around Rain's neck and twirled a finger in Rain's hair. "Sound like a plan?"

Rain allowed herself to be pulled into a soft, slowly deepening kiss. Francine's hands traced the back of Rain's neck and traveled lower, grazing her back and clutching her hips with a force Rain hadn't expected.

Francine could be very persuasive when she wanted to be.

The next morning, Rain studied her closet with an intensity usually reserved for the refrigerator at two a.m. "What does a person wear to a meeting with a possible mobster?"

"A wire?" Francine watched from her usual place on the left side of Rain's bed.

"Not helping." Rain felt trapped in a bad movie, reading from the wrong script. She shouldn't even be considering this. It was ridiculous. And yet, she knew she had to. He knew her real name *and* where to find her. Rain had spent many painstaking years attempting to erase her given name from the planet, going so far as to appeal to the court system to change it legally. In the eyes of the law, she was just Rain, but no one who knew her real name would ever let her forget it. Francine was the only person she'd ever told and that was under naked, handcuffed duress.

There was also the matter of the thousand dollars the pale man had left in the envelope. *Was it even real? Fucking hell, what if it was counterfeit? Should I even try to spend it? The whole idea is insane, but here I am, picking out what could possibly be the last thing I will ever wear.*

"Don't be so dramatic," Francine said, and Rain realized she'd been thinking out loud.

In the end, she settled on a plain, green button-down and yesterday's jeans, her favorite pair. They fortunately didn't smell too much like old food. Francine scrunched her nose at Rain's wardrobe choice, but Rain didn't care. If Rain was going to meet her maker, she'd do it wearing comfortable clothes.

The Dunkin' Donuts chosen by the pale man was on an exceptionally busy downtown corner. Rain had to circle the block twice to find metered parking. She couldn't afford the garage rates, at least not while unsure about spending the grand in her pocket.

Francine leaned against the corner of the building while Rain tried to peer through the wide window without being seen. The shop wasn't empty, but it also wasn't as busy as she would've hoped. A seasoned mobster could easily take out the few straggling, would-be witnesses. The pale man sat in the farthest corner from the door, clutching a Styrofoam cup. He looked up and met her gaze, erasing the chance for Rain to just walk away. Her stomach did a somersault.

"Oh, go on," Francine said from around the corner. "I'll be right here."

Reluctantly, Rain shuffled inside. A blast of warm air hit her like a wall, and she immediately began to sweat. The pale man looked just as uncomfortable. He tugged on the collar of his shirt, and an opalescent sheen covered his forehead, making him look pasty and unwell.

She sat down across from him and folded her hands in her lap to hide the fact that they were shaking. Rain thought about what Francine had said about wearing a wire and wondered if it really was as ridiculous a notion as it sounded at the time. For all she knew, there were FBI agents in here right now, and just by sitting across from the pale man Rain had implicated herself in whatever scheme he was planning. She should've bought a coffee or something. *Idiot.*

"Are you okay?" The pale man said.

Rain looked up from her folded hands. "Huh?"

"You were mumbling."

"Oh." She really needed to get a handle on her inner monologue.

The pale man visually appraised her, and the grimace shrouding his face implied she'd been found wanting. He reached into his jacket, and Rain flinched, crouching low in her seat.

The pale man sighed. "I'm not going to hurt you."

That's what they always said right before shooting you in the face, but Rain looked up anyway. In his hand, he held another envelope, identical to the first, and laid it on the table. She didn't know whether she should take it. "Is this some kind of test?"

"A test for what?"

Rain shrugged.

The pale man pinched the bridge of his nose. "I think maybe we got off on the wrong foot last night. Let me start over." He extended his hand over the table. His fingers were long, his nails short and yellow. "My name is Jude."

"Call me Rain." She took his hand and gave him a look that said she meant it. None of that *Rainfall* shit, thank you very much. "Are you with the mob?"

"What mob?"

"I don't know. *The* mob. Gunfire and favors and bosses."

Jude looked genuinely confused. Maybe he wasn't with the mafia. She had to admit it was highly unlikely the mob would operate out of the hipster capital of the Midwest. But then, who *was* he with?

"Right. Well, Rain, as I mentioned in the note, I have a job for you."

"I'm not a hooker."

Jude's hand shot forward, nearly knocking over his cup. "Ex—uh—excuse me?"

"You heard me. I know how this works, okay? I've got cable. The pastor or priest or whoever you work for is looking for a Miss-Love-Him-Long-Time on the side. Sorry to disappoint, but that's not happening." She crossed her arms over her chest.

"No. That's not—ugh." He massaged his temples in slow circles. "*Job* is probably the wrong word. It's more like a... like a role."

"What kind of role?"

Jude leaned forward over the table. His breath was like death. "How familiar are you with the New Testament?"

Rain sighed. These bible thumpers were getting weirder by the day. "Look, thanks for the offer... or whatever... but like I told you at the restaurant, I'm not interested."

She tried to stand but couldn't move. It was like her legs had been shackled to the booth. The blood drained from Rain's face. When she looked up, Jude was scowling.

"I need you to listen to what I have to say." His lips set in a tight line while he waited for her to acknowledge him.

She nodded.

He took a sip from his cup before pushing it to the side. "I don't know how you people can drink this shit. Anyway, the New Testament: the compendium of the life of Jesus of Nazareth as understood by the peoples of Earth. You ask me, it is seriously lacking in what we at Trinity like to call *fact*, but that's neither here nor there. The one bit you people got right was the promise of the Second Coming of Christ."

Jude paused as though he could tell Rain was only half-listening. She struggled to pull her legs from her invisible bonds and flicked her gaze to see if she could catch Francine's eye, but her roommate had her back to the window. He tapped the table. Rain's breath caught.

"This is important because that promise is about to be delivered. Has already been, in fact."

"And what the hell does that have to do with me?" Rain didn't like feeling trapped. Face hot, she had to bite her tongue to keep from grinding her teeth.

"You're it," he said, casually, as if he were telling her the time.

"I'm what?"

"You're the embodiment of the Second Coming of Christ. The Messiah."

Rain considered him a moment, looking for any indication that he was trying to be funny, but his face could've been made of marble. "You're out of your fucking mind."

This would've been an excellent time to get up and run as fast and as far as was humanly possible, but Rain still couldn't move. Her body hadn't quite caught up with her mind. Shock. Another second, and her flight instinct would kick in.

"I'm sorry to restrain you like this, but I don't have much of a choice."

Restrain? She wanted to scream but knew it wouldn't do any good. The other patrons would politely dismiss her as being batshit, and Francine was surrounded by Minneapolis traffic. There was no way Francine would hear. "Who... what are you?"

"I am a consultant with Trinity Corporation who has been... elected to serve as your agent in this journey."

"Is anything coming out of your mouth going to make sense?"

"Probably not."

Rain's head spun. It had to be some kind of hallucination brought on by Francine's cheap wine.

"This will be much easier if you just accept what I've told you so that we can continue." Jude checked his watch. "There's too much to accomplish to waste time in deluded denial."

"If I were what you say I am, wouldn't I know it?"

"Now you do."

Rain shook her head. "You're nuts."

"I get it. You want proof. No problem." He looked around before settling his gaze on the case of bagels next to the register. "See that pastry display over there?"

She raised her eyebrow.

"Multiply the bagels. Fill the trays."

"Excuse me?"

"Just focus on the case and imagine it full."

She tilted her head. "You're serious."

Jude's forehead crinkled, and his cheeks pinked. His patience seemed to be wearing thin. "Just do it."

Thinking he might lash out if she didn't play along and because she still hadn't figured out how he was keeping her rooted to her chair, Rain fixed her eyes on the case. Her stomach growled. She blinked, and suddenly, the case was filled with hundreds of golden-brown bagels. "Jesus Christ."

"Finally, we're getting somewhere."

"I actually did that?" Rain blinked again. She had to be hallucinating.

"Yes." Jude pushed the envelope closer to her. "Now, back to your role."

"That's unbelievable."

"Your role, Rain."

She snatched the condiment basket from the corner of the table. "Can I do it with sugar packets?"

Jude grabbed the basket away from her. "No."

"Why not?"

"Because."

"You sound like my mother."

He smacked the table. "And you're acting like a child!"

The background noise of the shop fell away. A few remaining patrons gaped at them.

Jude lowered his voice and craned his neck over the table. "This is not a joke, and it's not a game. So please try to take this seriously."

Rain felt whatever force had been holding her still lessen. He must have known she wasn't going anywhere. How could she? "But I'm not—I mean—I don't even believe in God."

Jude cringed and stole a glance upward. "Luckily, that isn't a prerequisite, but for this to actually work, you may want to rethink your position."

Rain shook her head. "This doesn't make sense. It's fucking surreal. I don't even know if I want to do it—whatever that entails. I don't think I can. You have the wrong girl."

"I told you in my note that this was an offer, implying that you had a choice, but the fact of the matter is, you don't."

She opened her mouth to object, but Jude shushed her.

"You'll need to quit your job, obviously." He touched the envelope on the table. "There should be enough in here to get you through until I come for you again so that we can get started."

"Started?"

"All in good time. I'll see you in a week."

"But—"

"Rain. Some advice? Don't think about it too hard. Just accept it, and continue with your day. Trust me." He stood. "One week."

Rain let him leave first as Francine told her to, though she doubted it would make any difference. If this guy was for real, he'd find her no matter where she was. When Rain neglected to follow his exit, Francine came inside and sat where Jude had been.

"So?"

"I need to find a Bible."

Francine's mouth fell open. "What did he say to you?"

"You wouldn't believe me if I told you. Hell, I don't really believe it."

"Tell me."

Rain shook her head and twirled the envelope. It felt heavy.

"What's in this one?"

"Same as the last, I think." Rain didn't dare open it here to confirm it. Too many nosy people around. Funny, a moment ago she'd been worried there weren't enough.

Francine pushed the envelope into Rain's chest and stood. "Well, then, let's get out of here."

Rain felt the burn of several pairs of eyes on her as she followed Francine out onto the sidewalk.

Jude had at least been serious about the contents of the envelope. Once safely inside the car (doors locked), Rain opened it to find another thick wad of cash, mostly twenties, that totaled fifteen hundred dollars. Two thousand, five hundred dollars to last her the week. What did they want from her that required they throw around money like this?

"I've never seen that much money in one place in my life," Francine said.

"Me neither."

"We ought to test it."

"How?"

Francine thought a moment. "Those pens we use at work to check the big bills."

Rain nodded and stuffed the bulk of the cash in her bra for safekeeping. She tucked a pair of twenties into her wallet. "We need to make a pit stop first."

They stopped at a Barnes & Noble on the way to Maxwell's. A large collection of Bibles in every shape, size, and binding possible engulfed the majority of the Religion section. Rain pulled a paperback copy, roughly the size and shape of a brick, from the shelf and thumbed through its pages. The sheer amount of text in the bible gave her gut-twisting flashbacks to her one disaster of a year at the University of Minnesota when she had been lucky enough to leave the dorm with pants on, let alone make it to class on time. She hadn't just failed, she'd bombed.

At the register, the cost came to eight dollars and change. She used Jude's money to pay, holding her breath as the cashier considered the bill. Pocketing the change, Rain ran from the bookstore.

She let Francine drive. The Bible felt heavy in her lap, and simply having bought it, implying that she might actually believe the load Jude had slung at her, left her nerves a little frayed. It felt awkward and wrong. Rain's earliest memory involving Christianity was an embarrassing lecture by her mother of the dangers of monotheistic religions and the *knuckle-dragging bigots it created,* all because she'd asked if she could go with a friend to Bible school over the summer. Rain had been seven at the time. She didn't care about the God part of it. She just wanted to see the puppet shows. Her friend had said they were the best in the whole world.

She didn't get to go to Bible school. Instead, her parents sent her to the Sisters of Our Mother Retreat: an entire summer of gnawing tree bark and boiling animal feces for medicine. Seeing the experience as a punishment for even alluding to the "G word," Rain never mentioned it again.

Her knowledge of the religion, as a whole, was unbelievably limited. She hoped that somewhere in the giant book in her lap would be some clue as to why *she* was suddenly being dragged into it.

At Maxwell's, Rain snatched the bill marker from the front desk and, with Francine trotting behind, walked directly into Joey's office where she unceremoniously shooed him out.

"What the hell?" Joey shouted from behind the closed door.

Francine threw the lock. "Keep your pants on. We'll be out in a minute."

Rain pulled the bills from her bra, damp with sweat, and spread them over the desk. She yanked the pen cap off with her teeth, and with an almost intimate degree of care, marked each bill with a delicate slash at their corners. She waited for the marks to scream yellow, indicating counterfeit bills. Instead, they faded to a deep brown.

They were real. Every bill, legit tender.

Rain could think of nothing to say except, "Holy fuck."

Francine squealed. "Oh, this is so noir."

Joey pounded on the door.

"Better pack it up before Meathead breaks the door down."

Rain rolled the bills, and back into the bra they went. The stress was making her sweat more than usual. She'd need to hang the bills out to dry if they spent much more time beneath her breasts. She adjusted the bills to a less pokey location and then opened the door.

Joey stood, arms crossed but with a twinkle in his eye. "And what exactly were you two doing in there that was so urgent?"

Francine pushed passed him, trailing Rain by the hand. "Quit being pervy, and get us a table in the bar. Rain's buying."

Francine ordered the first round while Rain retrieved the Bible from the car. She cracked the book open in her lap and sipped from the too-fruity concoction her roommate was partial to. Jude had said something about the New Testament, so Rain decided it was okay to dismiss the entire Old Testament, knocking her reading down by more than half. That was encouraging.

She began to read:

> **John 1:1** *He who was from the beginning, whom we have heard, whom we have seen with our eyes, upon whom we have gazed, and whom our hands have certainly touched: He is the Word of Life.*

This was going to be a long, long night.

Five fruity things and three books later, Rain was no closer to an answer. But on the bright side, she was thoroughly hammered, and that was almost as good. It became more apparent in Rain's fuzzy brain that Jude was fucking crazy, and that thing at Dunkin' Donuts was an elaborate ruse, probably with the help of that street magician who'd been getting so much hype for his trick of making the Sears Tower disappear. Maybe Francine had been in on it too. Her love of practical jokes often overshadowed things like tact and human decency. It was hard to think about. Rain needed food, and the kitchen would close for the night in an hour.

She reached across the table and stroked Francine's forearm. "Feed me."

Francine's eyebrow twitched.

"No. Food."

Feigning disappointment, Francine snatched a menu from a recently vacated table and held it open for Rain to look at. The words swam unmercifully fast, but it didn't matter. Rain knew the menu by heart, and there was only one decent vegetarian option.

"Black bean burger. Big one."

"You got it." Francine disappeared into the kitchen to give them the order.

The burger arrived shortly after, alongside a plate of cheese fries for Francine. Rain was about to cut the head-sized burger in half when she noticed something weird about the top bun. The sesame seeds were arranged in such a way that they produced an image that looked exactly like her face in profile.

I'm really *drunk.*

Or the guys in the back were having a laugh at her expense, but how could they know what Jude had told her? Then there was the fact that they were borderline retarded and probably couldn't draw a triangle if their lives depended on it. No, it couldn't have been them. Francine? No, Rain hadn't told her the details of the conversation, only that it was ridiculous. She rubbed her eyes and looked back at the bun. The image was uncanny.

Rain pushed the plate away. She'd lost her appetite.

CHAPTER FOUR

THE NEXT DAY, RAIN DROVE Francine to work. She wanted to give Joey the news that she was leaving in person.

"Why are you being so secretive about this whole Trinity thing?" Francine fumbled through her bag. "I thought you could tell me anything."

"I just want some more information first." Rain caught Francine glaring out of the corner of her eye. "I promise I'll tell you though. Soon."

"But you know enough to quit your job? He gave you a lot of cash but not enough to live on."

"I know."

"So tell me."

Rain shook her head. "Not yet."

They spent the rest of the drive in stony silence.

If there was one person on the planet who wouldn't tell Rain she was crazy for even considering that her being the Messiah was true, it was Francine. But voicing it aloud would only make it all the more real, and Rain would have to accept that either everything she'd ever thought she knew about the world was wrong or that she was on the fast track to the psych ward.

After meeting with Rain, Judas booked himself a room at a Motel 6 a few miles from her apartment. He showered and was able to scrub most of the corpse stench from his body. But traces of it lingered even after a second scrubbing with the motel's harsh soap. He dried and then studied his face in the mirror. Technically more than two thousand years old, Judas still couldn't figure out when he'd started to look like an old man.

He left the bathroom to find G sitting cross-legged on the bed.

"That went well." G's eyebrows furrowed.

Judas wrapped the towel tighter around his bottom half. "Checking up on me already? Where's the trust?"

"When you know as much as I do, trust is a luxury one can ill afford." G's gaze flickered to the towel. "Do you mind putting on some clothes?"

"You going to watch?"

G smirked, turning his face to the wall. "Not that this makes a difference. I see all, you know."

Judas dressed quickly, unable to shake the feeling of being leered at. "You really know how to make a guy uncomfortable."

"We all have our talents."

Sighing, Judas leaned against the wall. "So to what do I owe the pleasure of this visit?"

"As you said, checking up on you."

Judas rolled his eyes.

"And I wanted to get your thoughts on Rain."

"What do you mean?"

G shrugged. "How do you find her?"

"Honestly?"

"Obviously."

Judas crossed his arms. "I pity her."

"Poisonous thing, pity." G's expression softened. "Why?"

"She's spent her whole life thinking that Heaven and Hell were just bedtime stories, that her actions weren't compiled and analyzed on high for use in her final judgment. Ignorance, as they say, is bliss. Now?" He shrugged. "That's all gone out the window."

"Well..." G stood. "I suppose you should have thought of that before you suggested her name to me."

Judas grunted.

"Be careful not to get too invested. You know how this is going to end."

Judas's stomach turned.

Rain knew Joey would try to talk her out of quitting. Between Francine and Margo they could handle the slow season, but he'd have to hire someone new eventually, and that thought, she knew from experience, filled him with anxiety.

"Why do you need to quit again?"

"Personal stuff."

"You can't just drop to part-time or something? I'll work with you."

Rain shrugged.

Joey sighed. "Fine, but if this has anything to do with Francine, I'd rather fire her and keep you."

Rain and Francine's on-again, off-again was hardly a secret.

"I heard that!" Francine called from across the empty restaurant. *Ears like a dog, that one.*

"It isn't Francine. Like I said, I just have stuff I need to deal with. If I can, I'll come back once it's all dealt with, okay?"

That seemed to cheer him up. He patted her back. "Okay, then."

She hated giving him an empty promise. From what little she'd read of the first "Coming," Rain gathered this was pretty much a lifetime gig.

Rain spent the following few days at the library. She gave the Bible a shot, reading until her vision blurred. But then she considered peeling her face off with a spoon as a distraction. There had to be another option. Fortunately, she had the Internet. There had to be a CliffsNotes version out there somewhere.

It seemed everyone was a theologian when it came to Christianity. Rain spent hours clicking among six web sites, all claiming to be the "final" word on the interpretation of the New Testament. Two days into her research, she was no closer to the answers she wanted. Her search was too broad. On the third day, Rain narrowed her search to the phrase "The Second Coming." A rock settled at the bottom of her stomach as she clicked through the results. Each page agreed on one thing: the Second Coming would ultimately lead to the Apocalypse. Or as one article postulated, the Messiah would show up once the Apocalypse had already begun.

Rain rested her face in her hands and tried to keep her breath steady. She was jumping to conclusions. Jude would have brought that up, wouldn't he? No, she told herself. He wouldn't have. He wanted her to go along with the program without an argument.

She did another search for the term *apocalypse*. Each article that came up was accompanied by images of fire and destruction, people cowering in fear of the dark, oppressive sky.

This was the job? To bring about the end of the world?

There was no way Rain would be able to sort through all this crap on her own. She needed to talk to someone.

The first church Rain came to was St. Laurent of Cardiff, Catholic. The main building was small and in serious need of a coat of paint. The steeple, swaying slightly in the breeze, was covered in a spongy green moss. A bird-poop-splattered statue of St. Laurent hunched over a stone fox was the centerpiece of the property. She sat in her car, idling in the empty parking lot, trying to convince herself that there was no one in the building, so she couldn't possibly go inside. Ever since she'd been a child, she'd had this vision of crossing the threshold of a church and spontaneously combusting. Her procrastination tactic was working too, until a doll of a woman scuttled out leaning on a walker. The door whispered closed behind her, stopping just before it shut completely.

Reluctantly, Rain left her car and slipped into the church through the crack.

She expected to enter the main hall, or whatever they called it, but found herself in a sort of large foyer. A hallway led deeper into the building, and there was a multipurpose room off to the side. A sign advertising a Friday night fish fry fluttered beneath an air vent. Light shone from the opposite end of the hallway. Rain inched toward it, shushing the shrill cry of her mother's voice in the back of her head.

Distracted and a little afraid of possibly being struck by a bolt of lightning, Rain ran directly into a muttering old man in black. She bounced off his beach-ball-like middle.

"Bloody hell. Oh, sorry." The man straightened his white collar. "Can I help you, young lady?"

Rain hadn't been called a young lady since she'd been a kid, and it somehow sounded more demeaning in an Irish accent. She forced a smile. "I need to talk to someone."

"Talk or confess?"

Rain hesitated. "Confess?"

The man chuckled. "That sounds promising. Been a slow day. I'm Father Fitzgerald." He pointed to a pair of upright boxes next to a statue of woman in a blue cloak. Rain had read about her: the Virgin Mary. Crock of shit, if you asked Rain.

He continued, "You take a seat in the confessional on the left. I'll be in the one on the right in a minute. Strictly speaking, I'm not supposed to have seen your face, but I'll try my best to forget."

"Okay." Rain shut herself in the tiny box, feeling like an idiot.

She'd seen fictionalized confessions on television and knew that they either ended with some soul-shattering confession of murder, or the wall dividing the two boxes came away and something dirty happened. The latter was, by far, the more likely scenario. A person was expected to confess their most erotic secrets to a man who probably had a poster of Justin Bieber up in the rectory. She began to regret her decision to come to the church.

The floor of the confessional vibrated as Father Fitzgerald lumbered into the opposite box. A small panel slid open, and she caught a glimpse of his face.

"Don't look," he scolded.

Rain sat back against the wall. They both were silent for a moment.

"Never done this before, eh?" Father Fitzgerald said.

"That obvious?"

He snorted. "There's a script you follow, see? You say 'Bless me,

44

Father, for I have sinned,' then tell me how long it's been since your last confession. You can go ahead and just say 'never.'"

In one long breath, she recited, "Bless me, Father, for I have sinned. It has been never since my last confession."

"Are you here against your will?"

The question surprised her. "No."

"Fantastic." He clapped his hands. "Tell me then, child. Confess to me your darkest secrets." His voice took on a deep, movie-voiceover quality. "And make it good. Like I said, slow day, and I'm bored out of my mind."

This wasn't right. "Are you really a priest?"

"I really hope so. Otherwise, I've been missing out on more fun than I care to think about."

"Right." Rain squirmed in her seat. If he came through the door at full salute, she would have to hurt him, breaking some existential rule about violence against a man of the cloth.

"Anyway. Darkest secrets. Go."

Rain stole a glance at the panel to make sure his hands weren't making stroking motions before she spoke. "What do you know about the Apocalypse?"

"So no secrets then?"

"Question first, secrets after."

He mumbled incoherently then said, "Fine. Okay, the apocalypse takes place in the Bible in the book of Revelations." He paused. "Have you read the Bible?"

"Am I under oath?"

"Never mind. The apocalypse and following ascension will begin after the arrival of the Antichrist and the Messiah."

"Jesus, right?"

"Yes, Jesus. He was our first Messiah. There is some speculation as to whether the Second Coming will be Jesus of Nazareth as he was then or if his spirit will take another body."

Strike one against the doubt Rain clung to. "And does this person have to do anything? Could they, like, refuse to take part?"

"Refuse to bring about the great ascension? Seems like a pretty

45

selfish thing to do—selfishness not being a quality that the Messiah would have."

Tally in the other column. Rain could be selfish. Sometimes. An image of Francine rolling over in bed, obviously irritated, flashed in her mind.

Father Fitzgerald continued, "But I don't think he would have a choice in the first place. His Coming would be an event that set other events into motion, bringing about the apocalypse. It will happen around him."

"Or her."

He stifled a laugh, and Rain's face grew warm under a mix of anger and embarrassment. *Why couldn't a woman be the Messiah? Fuck him.*

"Hypothetically speaking, I guess."

She forced her frustration to take a back seat. She was here for answers, not to argue. "But couldn't this person refuse? Couldn't she give up the role pushed on her by some vampire-look-alike with greasy hair and continue on with her boring existence?"

"No," he said simply, though confusion tinged his denial.

Rain fanned herself with her hand. It was starting to get hot in the box. She wasn't going to get what she needed here. "I have to go."

"Oy! What about your half? This is a confession, not a Q-and-A session."

Childhood claustrophobia threatened to crush her. She had to get out of the box. Now. "Fine. You want a confession? I'm it. The One. Find a bunker because the apocalypse is coming."

She kicked the door open and stumbled out into the hallway. She stood, taking deep breaths, trying to force her anxiety back into hiding.

Father Fitzgerald calmly exited his side. He caught her eye. "Wait here." He disappeared into a room on the other side of the Virgin.

Jesus Christ, he's going to call the Vatican or something. I can't do this. What if they torture me? Exorcise me? Don't people die from that?

He returned, holding a card, and handed it to her, wearing a solemn expression. Rain took it and read.

Dr. Jeremiah King, PhD

Psychotherapist

Specialty in delusion disorders.

Rain tore it in half and threw it back at the priest. "Your funeral." She stormed out of the church.

CHAPTER FIVE

JUDE CAME FOR RAIN EARLY the following Sunday. Somehow, she knew he would and didn't sleep the night before. Francine stayed up with her, listening intently to Rain regale her with the story of her interaction with the priest. When Rain finally told her who Jude claimed to be and who she supposedly was, Francine laughed.

She laughed harder when Rain couldn't reproduce what had happened at Dunkin' Donuts.

"Performance anxiety." She'd patted Rain's leg.

Rain sneered.

Francine made an effort to contain herself. "Real or not, this is the most interesting thing that has ever happened to you. Just go with it."

"But what about the whole end of the world thing?"

Francine shrugged. "The world ended a long time ago, love. We're only just catching up."

It hadn't been a comforting notion, and the longer Rain stayed awake thinking about it, the more anxious she became. When the doorbell rang, she stood too quickly, and vertigo sent her reeling. She recovered her equilibrium and then answered the door. Jude stood with his arms crossed over his chest. He wore a blue suit this time, though that was the only difference. A crease cut into his forehead.

"Ready? You look like shit."

"Niceties are gone already? Charming." Rain stood to the side so that he could come in, but it was clear he wasn't moving. He expected her to leave now? "I didn't sleep much."

"The circles under your eyes look like shiners."

"You should see the other guy."

He rubbed his face. "We'll have to fix you before we go. Image is important."

"What happened to *come as you are?*"

Jude didn't answer immediately. "I've got some moisturizer in the car. We'll get you some strong coffee, too. We have to go now, or we'll be late." He turned and headed toward a sleek black sedan.

She could still refuse to go along with all of it. It could all be some freak show's schizophrenic episode. Or a joke. Or one seriously fucked up dream.

Jude yelled something from next to the car.

Here goes nothing.

The moisturizer Jude gave her was an unusual—and probably expensive—medicated cream that made her feel as if she'd just had a face lift. It bothered her less once she had coffee in her system.

Then Jude drove them onto the highway, and her calm shattered.

He drove like a sixteen-year-old who'd just scored a license and the keys to Dad's Oldsmobile. Rain groped the ceiling for the *oh shit* handle as he sped through traffic, weaving between cars and nearly clipping the corner of an eighteen-wheeler. She clutched her stomach, thankful she hadn't bothered with breakfast.

"You're gonna kill us."

Jude grunted and slowed slightly.

"Shouldn't we be traveling on the wings of angels or something?"

"Where did you come up with that bull?"

"I don't know. This just feels too normal."

"A week ago you were clutching *normal* like a baby blanket."

"I just mean…" Actually, Rain didn't know what she meant, so she switched gears. "Are you going to tell me anything about where we're going?"

"To make your debut as the Messiah."

The queasy feeling returned with a vengeance. "It's happening now? Is the world ending?"

Jude glanced at her, eyebrows raised. "I wouldn't have pegged you as an extracurricular research kind of person."

"Someone tells you that you're the Messiah of a religion with a God you don't believe in, it's hard not to wonder. Answer the question."

"The world's not ending."

Rain snorted. "So they're all wrong?"

"Yes." Jude sighed. "And no."

Rain held her breath. Jude was driving dangerously close to the car in front of them.

"The theory is right. We've decided to do things out of order. Call it a loophole."

"Meaning?" She pulled open the glove box.

Jude snapped it shut. "Without an Antichrist, there's no one for the Messiah to defeat. No fight, no End of Days."

"So then, what's the point of this?"

"Humans are jaded. Too jaded. The spirit of mankind under which it was originally created has been perverted by religious sects claiming to be in direct communication with God—hint: they're not—and extremists on the other side of the spectrum who stomp on any glimmer of faith, even if it's not faith in God. You people would give Lucifer's hordes a run for their money. You all hate each other and come up with new reasons every day to stoke that fire."

Shame wasn't the right word for how Rain now felt, but it was close. "You were human once too."

"Which is why I can say all that with any credibility. The point, Rain, is for you to show them what it means to be human."

It was early afternoon by the time they arrived at the Dorothy Day Center. Jude had gotten turned around and managed to take them fifty miles in the opposite direction of the city. Rain could've helped him avoid the whole fiasco, but no, he'd insisted on keeping her in the dark about everything.

Scattered over the property were nearly a hundred people, some dressed in layers and layers of clothing, all the same dingy gray color, and others wearing nearly nothing at all. The spring warmth had yet to cut through the remnants of winter. They huddled against one another, probably to share body heat. Rain zipped her jacket while Jude led her to the entrance. A hand-written sign was taped crookedly to the door. It advertised an eleven o'clock lunch and asked that volunteers check in at the office.

Walking through the door, Rain cringed against the onlookers' leers. She wondered why they hadn't come in out of the cold until a woman bounded from around the corner, waving her arms. She wore glasses that took up half her face and kept slipping down the bridge of her nose.

"I'm sorry, but you can't come in yet," she said in a poorly disguised tone of exasperation. "Ten minutes, then I promise I'll let you lot in."

Rain raised her eyebrow. Did she look homeless? Jude certainly didn't. She waited for him to say something to the woman, but he stood silently.

"I'm here to volunteer?" Rain looked up at Jude for confirmation. He nodded.

"Oh." The woman brightened. "Super. We're short today. I'm MaryAnn." She put out her hand.

Rain shook it. "Rain."

MaryAnn appraised Jude. He remained quiet. "Strong, silent type, eh?"

"His name's Jude."

"Parole officer?"

It had to be the hair. Francine always said Rain's haircut made her look like a fugitive.

"No. He's my agent."

MaryAnn narrowed her eyes. "We don't allow cameras in here. If you're here for your... image... it's a wasted effort."

"No," Rain said, irritated. "We just want to help."

"In that case, glad to have you both. I'll grab you a couple of nametags, and we'll head to the kitchen. The crowd will riot if we don't have the doors open at eleven."

With *Hello, My Name Is...* stickers taped across their chests, MaryAnn led Rain and Jude to a large hall filled with old picnic tables. The floor was scuffed linoleum, and the walls were painted cement blocks. At the front of the room, a hole had been cut in the wall to resemble a cafeteria serving station. MaryAnn escorted them behind the cutout where a table was lined with several foil chafing dishes filled with various cold cuts, fruit, and potato chips. The final one held a molten sludge MaryAnn called *sloppy joe stuff.*

"Jude, I'll have you at the front of the line manning the buns."

Rain snickered. *Manning the buns.*

"And Rain, we'll put you at the end here in charge of the sloppy joes."

Rain eyed the bubbling mess and tried not to breathe through her nose. The sauce was redder than it probably should have been, so it looked like the mutilated cow meat simmered in its own blood.

"Oops. Forgot the hairnets. Back in a jiff." MaryAnn rushed to the back of the kitchen.

Hairnets? Rain groaned.

Jude smoothed his hair back, apparently thinking the same. "When the people come to you, after you've served them—that—I want you to turn their water into wine."

"Sure, and while I'm at it, I'll shoot lasers from my eyes. You know, really make it a show."

"I thought we were past this whole doubt thing?"

"You should talk. Yeah, I saw the way you looked at me. Not exactly confident in my abilities, are we?"

He waved away her comment. "You have to believe that you can do it, and you will."

"Sounds like a crock."

"I agree." He adjusted his tie. "Doesn't make it any less true."

"And what if I can't do it? What if that thing with the bagels was a fluke?"

"It wasn't."

Rain scoffed. "I should have guessed this wouldn't just be about helping people."

Jude rolled his eyes. "We *are* helping them. You think they won't be grateful for a cup to drown their sorrows in?"

Rain wanted to argue further, but MaryAnn reappeared, mess of hair tamed beneath a hair net, carrying two more. Jude affixed his without comment. Rain decided she couldn't look any more ridiculous than him and pulled hers on. The elastic dug into her forehead.

Just before the doors were to open, a short, round man with slacks pulled too high over his gut joined them at the serving line. He carried a box of latex gloves.

MaryAnn clicked her tongue. "I always forget those. Sorry, Pastor Mike."

"Not to worry, not to worry."

Rain took the gloves he handed to her and slid them over her fingers. They were a size too big. Her palms began to sweat, making the latex cling like a condom.

The doors opened before introductions between Rain and the pastor could be made. A swarm of people banked around the tables and slid en masse into a line, grabbing trays, cups, and plastic cutlery. Several of the women had children attached to their hips and backs and handed them their own utensils. Even the kids looked like it was old hat to them. How depressing to know this place existed, and people really did live on the street with nothing to their name but a blanket and a box. Having it in her face made Rain feel guilty for just *existing*. Maybe Jude was right. They probably could use a drink. Rain wouldn't have minded a shot or two.

The first man to reach her station smelled like urine and held his tray with one shaky hand. A bottle of water shivered on the corner of his tray. Did she have to touch it, or could she just look at it? At Dunkin' Donuts, Jude had said that she just needed to envision it. Rain closed her eyes. When she opened them, the liquid in the bottle had turned a deep shade of red. The man didn't notice. He tapped his open bun with a dirty finger, leaving brown prints in the bread. Rain scooped the meat mess onto his bun, and it splattered backward over her hand. Thank God for gloves.

She looked down the line at Jude. He nodded encouragingly.

The next person in line might have been a woman. She had large, hanging breasts, but her mustache rivaled anything Rain's father could have grown. The woman's cup was already half-filled with a reddish liquid, so Rain couldn't know if it'd worked for her.

Soon, her pan of sloppy meat mess ran out, and Pastor Mike took it away for refilling. Across the room, a fight broke out. A man with matted blonde hair had gathered several bottles of the previously-water-now-wine from his comrades. Hugging them to his chest, he used a cane to bash people who stupidly tried to steal theirs back.

MaryAnn ripped off her gloves and yelled for the pastor.

Rain looked to Jude. He didn't seem worried, but panic bubbled in her stomach. It was only a matter of minutes before MaryAnn and Pastor Mike figured out what happened. She should've been happy, or at least not freaking out, because wasn't this the point? To prove to people who would listen that she was who Jude claimed she was? Something didn't feel right.

MaryAnn and Pastor Mike ran through the kitchen toward the pair of men now rolling on the ground. Pastor Mike yelled at the men while MaryAnn rolled up her sleeves and tried to pull the smaller of the two out of the fight. It wasn't hard. He'd probably swallowed most of the wine because his legs were like overcooked spaghetti.

Once the punching stopped, Pastor Mike grabbed one of the bottles from the man and sniffed it. His face purpled.

"What in God's name is this?"

"Showtime." Jude ripped off his hair net.

Rain gingerly removed her gloves and hair net, counting her breaths to keep the sudden dizziness at bay. Confrontation wasn't something she'd ever been any good at.

"This was your doing, wasn't it?" Pastor Mike pointed a pudgy finger at Jude. "Do you have any idea what you've done?"

MaryAnn confiscated every cup and bottle in the room while Pastor Mike spoke, sometimes having to pry them from white-knuckled fists.

Jude smoothed back his hair and spoke with a grandiose wave of his hand. "It was Rain's doing."

"You stupid—"

"Rain is the Messiah, returned to Earth for the betterment of mankind. She has turned this water into wine so that the world may celebrate."

Rain's cheeks warmed. Jude pushed her forward. God, this was worse than coming out of the closet. At least then, she'd been met with indifference. That wouldn't be the case this time. She managed a meek, "Yes," before keeping eye contact with Pastor Mike became almost painful. She thought a vein might explode in his forehead.

Pastor Mike's eyebrow twitched, and his jaw clenched. "I don't care who you say you are. There are alcoholics here, and you've all but put a gun to their head by dosing them. Were you planning to get the children drunk too? Have a little laugh at the expense of these people?"

One of the men from the fight said, "Shut it, you fat fuck. Let the woman give us her cheap wine. Long live the Messiah!" He fell back, giggling and coughing.

"I didn't realize—"

Jude hushed her. He tilted his head and then muttered, *fuck*.

"What?"

Then Rain heard it too. Sirens.

MaryAnn emerged from the corner, cell phone in hand. "Took me a minute to put two and two together, but I figured it out."

"What are you talking about?" Rain said.

"It was all over the news. Oh, you just wait." Then, to herself, "I wonder if there's a reward."

Rain knew this had been a bad idea. But could she just grow a pair and tell Jude that she wouldn't do it? No. What kind of Messiah could she be if she just did whatever anyone told her to? A shitty one, that's what kind. Dread filled her chest. She didn't know if they could arrest her for it. It wasn't as if they'd find a bottle of red wine on her.

Jude did nothing to calm her. His face was screwed up, and his eyes darted back and forth as though he were trying to catch the way out with a look.

Footsteps echoed in the hallway, and the door flew open. Six policemen stormed in with guns drawn.

The blood fell out of Rain's face, and she had to brace herself against the wall to keep from falling. Even Jude looked confused.

All this for giving out wine?

"Hands up!" The lead cop inched toward her.

Rain threw her hands up. Her whole body trembled.

"That's her, officer," MaryAnn said smugly.

"This is obviously some kind of misunderstanding," Jude said. Before he could continue, a second cop dove on Jude and threw him against the wall, cuffing him.

"What the fuck is going on?" Rain said.

"You claimed to be the Messiah, yes?" the lead cop said.

Jude spoke before she could answer. "Yes. She is. That's why this is a huge mistake."

Rain stared daggers into the back of his head. Jesus, was he trying to get her shot?

"No mistake here. You're coming with us."

He tucked his gun back in his belt—Rain still had four others trained on her head—and turned her around before wrenching her arms behind her back. He slapped handcuffs on her wrists. "You're under arrest for the bombing of the Econo Corporation building."

"What?" Rain and Jude said in unison.

"Lots of blood on your hands, girlie." The cop shoved her toward the door.

CHAPTER SIX

PERHAPS HE HADN'T THOUGHT THE plan through completely. *Don't berate yourself. No one can know everything.*

The holding cell was in a general state of disrepair. The cot dipped at the center where the springs had snapped, walls bled moisture and mold, and the toilet still held the evacuations of the cell's previous tenant.

"Did I do something wrong?" he asked the voice.

"Still trying to figure that out, Sunshine. Hold your fuckin' horses," the guard yelled from his desk in the hall.

Judas leaned his head against the cold, stone wall. No matter how he positioned himself on the cot, his body ached in protest. His skin felt stiff and leathery, and it hurt to move. Trading one pain for another, he stood and paced the length of the cell, stretching his legs and rotating his arms in an attempt to loosen the skin.

You look like a windmill.

"Don't you have other people to bother?"

"Yeah, as a matter of fact, I do. But it's your lucky day, Sunshine. Shut up, and maybe I'll get this paperwork finished in time for your release next millennia," the guard said.

You'll be out of here in a jiff.

"And Rain?"

The guard snorted.

That answered his question.

Rain. All things considered, Judas couldn't help liking her. He saw something of himself in her—the him before the Messiah came. Lying to her made a stone form in his gut. Dropping a few letters from his name had been necessary, of course. Even the most theologically ignorant people knew the story of history's greatest betrayer. But everything else? It didn't even make sense.

It doesn't need to.

He shook his head. The only thing he had control over was his part in it. All he had to do was get through it alive. Then he could die in peace. Judas dropped his voice to a whisper. "You've told me everything, right?"

Of course.

The hairs on his neck rose. Never let it be said that deities didn't lie.

The Messiah, as it turned out, was a woman matching Rain's height and description who had blown up the main building of Econo Corporation's headquarters, along with several other pesticide producing plants over the last few months, leaving behind cryptic messages about the inevitable apocalypse if these plants were allowed to produce their "poisons."

Detective Park told Rain all this as she spread gruesome photographs over the table in front of her. The detective paced the perimeter of the small room, making the walls appear to close in tighter.

"I didn't do all that," Rain insisted. "It wasn't me."

"Way I hear it, you all but gave a confession."

Rain clenched her jaw so tight it hurt. "If I did, you'd have me booked by now, wouldn't you? I'm telling you I had nothing to do with it. Ask anyone."

"We're working on that, yes. But as it stands, the evidence is pretty compelling. Hard to believe it's a coincidence that someone looking exactly like this sketch"—Detective Park flashed a police sketch. The hair, mouth and eyes were the same, but the nose and jawline were way off—"happened to claim the same moniker as the bomber."

Rain sat back and folded her arms over her chest. Did this woman seriously believe that she was the woman in the sketch? There must have been a thousand women with similar features. Where the fuck was Jude, and why hadn't he gotten her out of here yet?

"If you cooperate with us, give us a full written confession, I might be able to persuade the DA to recommend a shorter sentence."

The surreal quality of it all was too much. "Fuck off."

The door opened, and the police officer who had arrested Rain entered, frowning. "Cut her loose," he said to the detective.

"Why?"

"Got a coupla people here by the names of Francine DuBois and Joey Martin with an alibi for Miss Johnson."

The detective looked back at her. Rain smiled widely.

"Fine." The detective shoved the police officer out of her way. She looked back to Rain. "This isn't over."

When the detective was out of sight, Rain stood.

"This way." The officer directed Rain to the front of the station.

Joey sat in the corner with his head against the wall. Francine paced the room, hair thrown into a hasty bun with escaped tendrils whirling around her face. When she saw Rain come through the security door, she ran to her and hugged Rain tight enough to stop blood flow.

Rain kissed her cheek. "How'd you know to come down here?"

"Jude told me."

So he *had* gotten out already. The bastard had just let her sit in that tiny room with Detective Stick-Up-My-Ass barking at her for hours.

"Let's go home," Rain said.

"Jude asked me to tell you to meet him—"

"Fuck Jude. I've just been accused of murder. I'm not going anywhere except my bed with a large glass of something liver-destroying."

Joey stood up and patted Rain's back. "It'll be okay, kid."

"Thanks, Joey."

He nodded and exited ahead of them, holding the door.

Rain shed her clothes, leaving a trail from the kitchen to the bathroom where she turned the shower on to its hottest setting. The room quickly filled with steam. She stepped under the stream and winced against the hot water. It burned, but the heat and pulse of the showerhead kneaded the knots in her back and shoulders.

If this was what Rain had to look forward to as the Messiah, then she wanted no part in it. Money and consequences be damned. Jude's idea of helping people had blown up in her face. He could find someone else. Rain wasn't cut out for the whole "sacrifice for the greater good" shit anyway.

She braced her hands against the wall and leaned forward, letting the water beat on her lower back.

The curtain slid open, and Francine stood wearing only a smirk. "If you wanted it like that all you had to do was ask, ya know."

Rain stood to make room for Francine in the small shower. Francine turned away, letting the water saturate her hair and fall over the fierce curve of her hips. Rain loved the little dimples in Francine's back.

Francine reached back and grabbed Rain's wrists, pulling her arms around her slight frame. Once Rain's hands were on Francine, it was impossible to stop touching her soft, velvety skin. Goosebumps prickled Rain's arms and chest. She kissed the back of Francine's neck at the center of a set of wings. The tattoo was a target for her lips.

Francine covered Rain's hands with her own and guided them in opposite directions. Rain traced the button of her nipple with her fingertip, feeling Francine arch her back and press her ass against her. She spread her legs to let Francine grind against her, a moan escaping her lips. God, she loved this girl's ass. Soon Rain's hand found the soft strip of down between Francine's legs, and she ran her finger along the outside. Her clit hardened under Rain's gentle strokes. Francine's legs trembled, and Rain couldn't take her own teasing any longer. She slid her fingers inside. Both gasped.

Rain rubbed herself against Francine while she fucked her with her fingers, biting her shoulder as tension pulled at her muscles. A guitar string ready to snap. Nails dug into the soft part of her thigh, sending throbs of excitement up her body.

"Faster," Francine said.

A growl erupted from Rain's throat. Francine thrust against her hand, panting. Water poured into Rain's eyes, but she forced them open to watch Francine.

Finally, she shuddered, and Rain cried out with her own pulsing orgasm under water that had gone cold. She held onto Francine, leaning against the wall of the shower, her legs refusing to support her weight. Her head spun.

Rain reached over and turned off the icy water then kissed Francine's ear.

"Did you like that?" Francine pried herself out of Rain's embrace.

Rain tried not to take the immediate brush-off personally. A post-fuck cuddle wasn't Francine's style. "Yes."

"Good."

Once Rain dressed and ventured into the living room, Francine had already carved out a place in the couch, legs draped over the arm, with the TV on. A pair of plastic cups sat on the floor, filled with the cheap whiskey from the back of the cabinet. Rain could smell it from the doorway.

In the dim, flickering light of the screen, Francine seemed to glow. It was in moments like this when Rain dared to wonder why they were never able to make it work as a couple. They'd tried—and tried and tried—but Francine would always have her secrets, and Rain would always resent them.

Rain didn't think she would ever stop caring for her though. She maybe even loved Francine, but she chose to keep such feelings buried as deep as possible. If Francine so much as suspected the L bomb, she would disappear for good.

Rain picked up one of the cups and sat at the opposite end of the couch, glancing up at the TV. "The news?"

"I wanted to see if they would show that sketch that they claimed looked exactly like you."

"It looked a little like me. Not a dead ringer, though." Rain paused. "I'm not doing this anymore."

"Not doing what?"

"You know what I mean."

Francine sighed. "I know it's scary, but—"

"No, Francine, you don't. It's too much, okay? Fucking Christ, I was accused of murder! You should have seen the look on that detective's face. She really believes it was me, no matter where you and Joey say I was. If I keep claiming to be the Messiah..." Rain laughed.

The Messiah. Jesus Christ. She laughed harder to keep from crying.

"You're not *claiming* anything. You *are*." Francine turned up the volume on the TV.

A plastic-looking female reporter stood in front of the Dorothy Day Center. Next to her was the homeless man from the kitchen disaster who had shouted, "Long live the Messiah." His face was cleaner, but from the sneer at the corner of the reporter's face it was obvious his stench was just as ripe.

Rain covered her face with her hands and groaned.

Francine pulled Rain's hands down and held them in her lap. "Just listen."

The reporter held the microphone up to the man's mouth. "It's a hard life out here, ya know? People look at ya like yer some piece of *bleep*. Can I say *bleep* on the air?"

"No." The reporter smiled nervously.

"Oh, sorry. Anyway, yeah, this girl? The pastor and his floozy gave her a hard time, but I thank her from the bottom of my heart, not just for the wine—and it was damn good wine, some vintage primo vino—but for giving me something I can look back on and laugh about. Don't get to laugh much out here."

The reporter signed off, and Francine lowered the volume again. "See?"

"I got him drunk. Anyone would be happy about that."

Francine smacked the back of Rain's head. "You never listen properly. You made him happy. Did you see that smile? That was hope."

Rain wanted to deny it, but she couldn't. It was obvious that, for a little while anyway, that man would walk with a spring in his step, thinking about the girl with the magic trick and the chaos it caused.

"If you want to," Francine continued, "you can give that to more people. To everyone."

Rain raised her eyebrow.

"Okay, so maybe not everyone, but *some* people. Isn't that enough?"

Rain thought about the detective again, about the clamminess of the room and the debilitating fear that she was going to be arrested for something she had nothing to do with. She wasn't an idiot. She knew things like that were going to continue to happen and possibly get worse. Thanks to the religious zealots of the last decade, anyone who claimed to be doing "God's Work" was met with immediate suspicion and anger. What she'd given to that man wasn't worth it. Yet. But it could be.

That night, Rain didn't sleep. Each creak in the ceiling or nocturnal creature outside her window was a gun-toting SWAT team member waiting for the right time to put a bullet in her brain. She tried to be rational, but what was rational about a person with a clean record—not even so much as a parking ticket—being hauled in for murder? No, more than that. It was terrorism. It didn't take a genius to figure out how they treated suspected terrorists. Could they still crucify people? *Sure,* a little voice told her, *if they keep it on the down low.*

Francine snored blissfully next to her, but Rain gave up the idea of rest when the sun came up. Careful not to disturb Francine, she rolled out of bed and dressed.

Daylight purged Rain's psyche of only a few of the things that were making her anxious. She needed to get out of the apartment.

As she drove out of the subdivision and into the first shopping center she came across, it occurred to Rain that there were few places open at dawn. One, in fact: a boutique café she'd never frequented. Her practical mind couldn't justify spending more than a couple of bucks on a cup of coffee. Now, thanks to Jude, Rain figured she could spare it.

Coffee and a blueberry bagel. Ten dollars gone, but the coffee was like silk going down, and the bagel tasted like nothing she'd ever had. Rain planted herself in a far corner of the shop, away from the crowd.

She'd forgotten that people did actually get out of bed before noon. But then, coffee had magical powers that turned zombies into working middle-class Americans in less time than it took to get through the morning commute.

Jude wanted her to show people what it meant to be human. As far as Rain knew, this was it: caffeinate, work, caffeinate again, home, a glass of wine, bed, or some other combination of the above. Rain knew that wasn't what he'd been going for. The human condition was meant to be more, that *more* being constantly speculated on by the religious, non-religious, and everyone in between. And everyone thought they had it right. Did any of them come close? Or were they all wrong? And how the hell was Rain supposed to understand it well enough to show them? She slumped in her chair as the weight of the world planted itself firmly on her shoulders.

Dregs swallowed, Rain refilled her coffee—she deserved it, thank you very much—and got in her car, not especially eager to get back to the apartment. The idea of a roof and walls was stifling.

She drove, not really knowing where she was going. Despite the cold, she rolled all her windows down and relished the feel of the wind on her face and neck. Breathing fresh air diluted some of the darkness inside. She didn't want it to end. *There has to be a park or something around here.* A quick route correction brought her to the only park in the neighborhood. It was a bit of an eyesore with the play equipment in disrepair and the ground littered with trash, but it was quiet.

A bench sat partially hidden beneath a flowering tree. Its branches hung low, like a curtain, its new green burden heavy on the winter-ravaged wood. Rain sat, hugging herself against the cold.

A jogger strode past in black and neon spandex. She watched, trying to summon some kind of empathy for the woman.

I don't even like people, Rain thought, *and now I'm supposed to be their savior.*

She pictured all the terrible things that could happen to the jogger before returning home: a mugger, a twisted ankle, a freak blizzard. All those things sucked, sure, but did Rain care? Not really. Tomorrow, Rain would forget all about her. The jogger would slip out of Rain's life like a shed hair, unnoticed and unmissed.

A group of small children stormed the jungle gym. Rain watched them with waning interest, finding it difficult to focus on the raw potential and innocence that she was supposed to be able to see in each child. Nothing. *Maybe I'm a sociopath.*

Directly across the park, on the opposite side of the jungle gym, a man leaned against a light pole. He seemed to appear out of nowhere, not that Rain would've noticed him approach over the kids' shrieks. The man was big, pro-wrestler big, and crossed his arms, maximizing his intimidation factor. He wore sunglasses, so Rain couldn't be sure if he was looking at her, but it felt as though he was. Her skin crawled.

She waited several minutes for him to look in another direction or, better yet, just fucking leave already, but he only stared. The man didn't flinch, didn't even seem to breathe, but steam began to rise off his back and the top of his head.

The woman who'd accompanied the children had noticed him too. Her gaze flicked between Rain, the man, and the children. Rain stood. The man took a step toward her. The woman sprinted across the playground. With each step, her body glowed brighter and brighter. Nose to nose with him, her skin shone a brilliant white.

Rain squinted. The woman shone like a human light bulb. It burned to watch her, but Rain was transfixed. The woman ripped the sunglasses from his face, and the breath caught in Rain's throat. His eyes weren't eyes but black holes. The woman looked directly into the black holes as she slammed her fist into his throat, dropping him. The man held his throat with one hand and groped at the woman with the other. She stepped on it, grinding her heel into his knuckles.

The man howled.

The woman planted a final kick to his face, and the man exploded in a fiery ball. The heat of it bowled Rain over, shoving her into the bench. She shut her eyes and clutched her chest. Her heart beat so hard it felt it might explode too.

When Rain finally felt that she was physically capable of handling it, she opened her eyes. The woman no longer glowed, but she was looking at Rain. A playful smile danced on her face.

That smile. She'd seen it somewhere before.

Rain drove home white-knuckling the steering wheel. Cold sweat stung her eyes, but she couldn't make herself blink it away. The woman had killed him. No. *Obliterated* him. And the way the woman looked at her? Rain wracked her brain trying to figure out where she'd seen her. It was more than just a passing familiarity. Rain felt it.

And the man. Well, he obviously hadn't been a man. Had he? *Demon* crossed her mind, but she swatted it away before it could take root because that would just be too damn much insanity for one morning.

Fuck.

She pulled into the parking lot, not giving a shit if she was in a parking spot, and ran upstairs where she put a pot of coffee on and unearthed the bottle of whiskey from the other night.

CHAPTER SEVEN

RAIN HAD BARELY TOUCHED HER coffee when Jude barged into the apartment, flustered and muttering, "... working conditions... expect me to..."

"On this planet, it's customary to knock before entering someone's apartment." She glared over the rim of her mug.

Jude looked at her as though he were surprised to see her there. "Sorry." He zeroed in on her sweatpants and bare feet. "You're not ready."

"Considering I had no idea you'd be gracing me with your presence this early, no, I'm not."

"Well, you should have assumed. You were supposed to meet me yesterday—"

Rain's voice rose. "Yesterday you let me rot in an interrogation room."

Jude stiffened.

"I deserved a few hours of peace after that."

He pinched the bridge of his nose. "Fine. Okay. But you need to get dressed. We're late, and if we get any later, we're screwed."

"No, *you're* screwed." Rain was in no mood for playing nice.

His face reddened, and his nostrils flared. "I'll meet you outside." Throwing open the door, he shook his fist at the sky and yelled, "Do you see what I'm dealing with?"

The door slammed shut behind him.

Francine emerged from Rain's bedroom, hair like a bird's nest and eyes only partially open. "The hell was that?"

"Jude is having a hissy fit."

Francine nodded. "Mm. Yeah, he does that." She disappeared back into the bedroom.

Rain swallowed the dregs of her coffee, dropped the mug into the sink and—

Wait.

She went to the bedroom and flung open the door. "Francine?"

Francine moaned from beneath a nest of pillows.

"Francine." Rain kicked the side of the bed.

"What?"

"What did you mean by, 'he does that'?"

"Huh?"

"Just a minute ago."

"I don't know. Maybe I was sleepwalking. Go away, I'm exhausted."

Francine wasn't sleepwalking. Another secret to add to the ever-expanding pile. There wasn't time to overthink it, though. *Late, late, late like the fucking white rabbit.*

Jude was already in the car with the engine running. He threw it into reverse before Rain had both legs inside.

"Jesus." She buckled her seatbelt and gripped the *oh shit* handle above the window.

"You think you could tone down the naming in vain?"

"Stop giving me a reason to invoke divine intervention. You're doing twenty over the limit."

"Late."

"Just like the other day? Maybe it's your poor planning that's the problem."

Jude ignored her.

Rain closed her eyes and forced her body to unclench. Francine had taught her a Lamaze-style breathing technique for dealing with stress, but after a few seconds of rapid, shallow breaths, Rain's head spun, and her stomach turned.

"Nearly there."

And no wonder: the speedometer needle twitched between 120 and 125 miles per hour.

Please don't let me die.

The car lurched and slowed, throwing Rain forward. She felt something crack. When she looked back at the speedometer, the needle sat at a sensible 55 miles per hour.

"What in the—?" Jude floored the gas pedal, but the car refused to accelerate. A line of cars backed up behind them, their drivers honking and waving. Reluctantly, Jude moved out of the fast lane, bringing the car behind a Buick that looked more like a boat. Its owner's tuft of gray hair was just visible over the seat back.

Jude shot Rain a panicked look. "What did you do?"

"What? Nothing." Hadn't she?

He didn't seem convinced. "I'll deal with it later. This is our exit."

The hospital's visitor parking was nearly empty. Rain figured it was still a bit early for visitors' hours to have started, which begged the question: why had Jude brought her here claiming to be late? Not that asking would do any good. He was just as bad as Francine.

An ambulance wailed a short distance away, getting closer.

They walked in through the front door, and rather than checking in with the nurse, Jude led Rain to the waiting area. "Sit."

She sat. "Now what?"

"We wait."

"Late, my asshole."

"Do you kiss your mother with that mouth?"

"Not since I was ten. We don't exactly get along."

"Oh, it's impossible to see why." He rolled his eyes.

"She's not a real picnic either. During a fifth grade field trip to the zoo that she volunteered to chaperone, my mother hijacked the school bus—holding the driver at bay with a Taser—and took us to a facility where they were supposedly testing makeup products on rabbits."

Jude's eyes widened.

"Yeah. She was arrested and all that, but it didn't stop her from being insane. The last time I talked to my sister, she said that Mom was harboring a dozen illegals in her basement, but that was almost five years ago." Rain picked up an old gossip magazine from the chair beside her and thumbed through it. "What about you?"

"What about me?"

"I don't know. Anything. The only information I have is your name. And not even that. A first name and last initial." Yep. That was it. A name and some cash and Rain had gone along with the program, basically no questions asked. God, when had she become so phenomenally stupid?

"I like to sleep."

"Oh, come on. Give me something that isn't completely irrelevant."

Jude shrugged. "There isn't much to tell. Up until recently, I served time in this... room, and now I'm here."

"Served?"

"Served. Spent. Whatever."

Rain rolled her eyes. "The winner for most ambiguous answer goes to..."

"Well, what do you want to know?"

"I don't know." She picked at her fingernails. "What are you, exactly? An angel or something?"

He recoiled. "No. Definitely not."

She raised an eyebrow. "Aren't angels... good?"

"Define 'good.'"

"I didn't think there was room for interpretation when it came to celestial beings."

"There's always wiggle room. Some people are just too narrow-minded to..." Jude blushed, and his jaw tightened. "And anyway, they're not good or bad. They just are: sexless, phantasmal servants to God who can be more than a little annoying in their infinite patience." He paused. "Well, except the Grigori. They were designed like humans in order to get close to them. To watch and protect them. That's what we call them: watchers."

"Are they still here?" She looked around in case one might jump from behind a chair and wave.

"Yes. But they're not exactly on the best terms with the rest of us. See, during the Fall, the Grigori thought it'd be fun to get involved with the humans. They developed romantic relationships. Had children. It was a giant mess. Their sexual partners started to see things they shouldn't have."

"Like?"

"Think about it. What is it the watchers would be watching?" He pointed downward.

"Demons?" *Like at the park?*

Jude nodded. "Scouts. Troublemakers. Anyway, when the dust settled after the war, the Grigori were left on earth to fade out of existence. They wanted to be close to humanity, so God granted them mortality. There are a few we keep in contact with, though, who were excluded from this… gift… Their knowledge is useful. Some continue to guard humanity out of habit."

He told her all of this with a straight face. Even with proof—if you could call it that—Rain found it all hard to digest. Jude expected her to change sides, like flipping a switch. She didn't know if she could. "Tell me about God."

"Tall order."

"Is God a man or a woman?"

"Neither. And both. Depends on the day."

The corner of Rain's mouth twitched. "Queer?"

Jude laughed. "No. Just not confined to biological gender."

"Tell me more."

"Like what?"

"Like what happened between the Old and New Testaments of the Bible? In the Old Testament, He… She… is fucking insane. Everything's on fire, death of the firstborn, locusts. Then the New Testament is like a wine and cheese party. Well, until that Judas guy pulls his shit and ruins everyone's lives." She stopped. Jude's face took on an ugly shade of green. "You okay?"

"Fine," he spat.

Minutes passed in silence.

Jude approached the reception desk. When he returned, he said, "Do you want some coffee or something? Looks like we have more time to kill than I thought."

"Sure."

While he was gone, Rain took yet another moment to weigh her options. Demons. The End of the World. Jude said it had been handled, whatever that meant, but there had been a demon in the park this morning. That couldn't mean anything good.

The woman who'd killed it—was that even the right word? Killed?—had to be one of those watchers Jude mentioned. She hadn't looked like an angel, just a woman. Rain focused on her face, trying to place it. She rested her forehead in her hands. Her eyelids grew heavy, and she began to drift…

Her room is messy. Mom will be mad. She'll get stuck in the box again. Rain hates the box. Sticky and smells like her brother's feet. Footsteps on the stairs. Rain hides under the blanket, which also smells like Sycamore's feet.

Screaming. Hitting.

Is that the doorbell?

Voices.

Another woman.

She sounds nice. Rain wants to see her face because nice voices don't always mean there's a nice face attached to it. She creeps into the hall. The voice is talking to Mom.

She's glowing.

The acrid stench of old coffee woke her. Jude held a cup of the stuff directly beneath her nose.

"They didn't have any sugar or cream, and I'm pretty sure this was brewed sometime yesterday."

The first sip was bitter and burned her tongue. The second, less bitter.

"Thanks."

The woman behind the reception desk waved, and Jude nudged her shoulder. "Finally. Let's go."

He thanked the woman with a nod as they passed the desk and jabbed a button on the elevator.

Inside, Rain tried not to inhale the sharp, antibacterial sting that seemed to be embedded in the walls. The elevator doors opened to reveal a long, wide, white hallway made brighter by flickering fluorescent lights. They passed several closed doors before stopping in front of a door, cracked open enough to reveal the shadow of a figure lying in a small bed. Voices spoke in hushed, haggard tones.

"So what are we doing here?"

Jude took a breath. "Okay, the first thing you need to remember is not to scream."

Her heart jumped. "Scream?"

"It's rude and will get us thrown out in a heartbeat. Don't do it. The second thing to remember is that you can heal this man."

"Heal?"

He nodded. "Ready?"

"Fuck no."

"Good enough."

Jude opened the door, and Rain struggled to swallow the scream expanding in her chest. A pair of women stood next to the bed, clutching each other and sobbing silently. They could have been twins except for the dramatic height difference. Sisters? On the bed lay a man mummified in gauze and bandages. The few exposed parts of him—face, neck, and one forearm—were pocked with gaping, purulent wounds, green and bloody. Despite the many bouquets of fragrant flowers placed strategically around him, the smell of flesh and decay was overwhelming. Rain wanted to cover her nose, but Jude seemed to read her mind and shook his head.

"You don't look like a priest," the man said to Rain, his voice strained and raspy. To Jude, he said, "You do. Kind of." He looked at the woman. "I said to get me a priest."

Jude gave Rain a shove forward.

She stifled a gag. "I, um, I think I can help you."

"You think, eh? How encouraging. This little girl thinks she can help me." He started to laugh, which turned into a bone-rattling cough. "Unless you're here to climb up on this dick before it falls off—"

One of the women cleared her throat.

"It already fell off?" His voice reached an impossibly high pitch.

"Half," she whispered.

"God dammit." He looked to Rain. "Guess you can't help me."

The taller sister stepped forward. "If there's anything you can do.

Please. They cured the leprosy, but it opened him up to necrotizing fasciitis."

Rain took a step back, dragging Jude by his collar, low, so that his ear was almost touching her lips. "You brought me into the same room as a leper? What the hell is wrong with you?"

"You heard her. They cured the leprosy."

"Oh, because flesh-eating bacteria is so much better."

She didn't consider herself particularly squeamish, but the idea of contracting a disease she'd only heard about on medical dramas made her acutely aware of every exposed inch of skin on her body and each germ-ridden breath she took. Rain doubled over, trying to protect her internal organs from skin-seeping parasites.

"So heal him. Then there won't be any necrotizing... whatever... left to get you."

"You're an ass."

"And you're the Messiah," he whispered, "So get to Messiah-ing."

"Still here," the bedridden man said.

Rain looked up, blushing. "Sorry."

"Did he say you could heal him?" the tall sister asked.

"Yes, she can." Jude yanked Rain's shoulders back so that she was standing straighter.

The woman's face brightened. She smiled at Rain. "Are you a specialist? The doctors here said they'd exhausted all options."

"She don't look like a doctor," the man said. "Too little."

"I'm not—"

"And that hair. Sheesh."

Rain ground her teeth. "No, I'm not a specialist." She paused. Jude kicked her ankle. "I'm the Messiah."

The women fell back into a single chair, legs twisted around each other to fit and hands over their faces. The short one sobbed while the tall one shook her head, mumbling. Her ramblings grew louder until she was screaming into her hands. When she removed them, her face was red and slick with angry spittle.

"Get out," she seethed.

Rain didn't have to be told twice. She turned on her heel and made for the door. Her hand clutched the knob.

The man said, "Please, don't go."

She turned to face him, expecting to see some kind of pleading glow about his face. There was a glow, all right, but only because he'd sat up, pulling the heart monitor toward him, and the screen struck light across his face. His smile was wide, revealing unnervingly white teeth. "Please," he said again. "I haven't had this kind of entertainment in months."

"I'm not a fucking clown," Rain said.

"No, no, of course not." The man struggled to contain a giggle.

Why couldn't Jude have found a nice nine-year-old with cancer for her to heal? Why did it have to be the asshole whose face was falling off?

"I can heal you but only if you drop the attitude."

"Ooh, sass! I thought the Messiah was supposed to be forgiving and humble."

"Fine. If you don't want my help, I'm out of here. Jude."

"Wait." The man raised his arm and flinched against the pain.

Rain raised an eyebrow.

"I..." He stopped, and his features fell. The light dimmed in his eyes, replaced by the hopelessness and anger it'd hidden. In his face, Rain saw every treatment that didn't work, every positive thought destroyed by new symptoms, the countless calculations of time—how much was his and how much had been taken by the disease—and the fear of what would happen should he allow himself to hope again.

Rain kept her distance. With his movement, some of his sores had begun to ooze. "What's your name?"

"Keith."

"What do you do?"

"I lay in bed all day."

Rain took a step toward the door.

"Okay, okay. Jeeze. I was a newspaper editor before I got sick."

"Did you like it?"

"It was fine. Why does this matter?"

It didn't. Rain was stalling. She'd tried to focus on him and picture him as healed, but it wasn't working. She'd stopped breathing, hoping to increase her concentration. She held it until her pulse thumped behind her eyes, and her chest ached. Imagination wasn't going to do it this time. Somehow Rain knew that she was going to have to touch him.

"Just curious." She inched toward the bed.

The sisters had stopped crying and watched with their arms wrapped around each other.

Did there have to be skin-to-skin contact, or would placing her hand over the bandages do the trick? There had to be gloves around here. Maybe she could get away with wearing those? When she stood directly over him, Rain realized there wasn't much skin to work with. The patches that hadn't been wrapped in gauze were greasy with some kind of protective gel.

She couldn't bring herself to actually touch his skin and rationalized that divine power had to be strong enough to penetrate cotton gauze. Just to be safe, she looked for the area with the thinnest amount of the stuff. Skin crawling and heart pounding, she placed her right hand on his chest.

"If you're going to touch me, do you think you could—"

"Shut up."

Rain closed her eyes and imagined the bacteria as little blindworms with vampire teeth and spines like a stegosaurus. Warmth spread through her body as she imagined a microscopic hammer crushing each one, their mutilated worm bodies being swept away by the now clean blood through his system.

The women's screams pierced Rain's ears. She opened her eyes, and her jaw dropped. The visible patches of Keith's skin were clear of sores. Pink scars had taken their place.

Son of a bitch. She'd healed him. *Unbelievable.*

"What?" Keith said. "What happened?"

Rain looked down at her hands, expecting to see them covered in sores. Her palms were redder than usual but otherwise looked perfectly normal. She felt a little weak, but she blamed that on the bad coffee.

Keith lifted a shaky hand to his face. Touched his neck. Looked at his forearm. He looked at Rain. "Holy fucking shit."

"You're telling me."

He pulled the IV from his arm and yanked the monitor patches from his hand. It took him a moment to find his balance on two feet, but once he was stable, Keith ceremoniously unwrapped his bandages.

He shot a look at the women. "Don't just stand there. Help me."

It took some time to de-mummify him, but the result was extraordinary. The sores had all been healed, and between his legs hung his bait and tackle, intact.

"It's bigger." He looked up at Rain with a mischievous grin.

"Don't look at me."

He strode across the room in three long steps, and before Rain had time to react, Keith hugged her. His dick rubbed against her hip, and she stifled a gag.

"Thank you." He kissed the top of her head. "Thank you, erm, Messiah?"

"Call me Rain."

Jude gripped her hand and pulled her from Keith's embrace. "Time to go."

"Thank God," she said. "I need a shower. And maybe some bleach."

Even so, Rain couldn't help being overwhelmed by a sense of pride. It was like the feeling she got from occasionally buying coffee for a stranger but on steroids. She positively beamed. Until she looked up at Jude's ashen face. Bags puffed under his eyes. He looked scared.

Jude must have felt her eyes on him. He forced a smile but didn't return her glance. "Listen, I've got an unexpected thing I've got to take care of. I'll take you home, but don't go anywhere until I come back for you, okay?"

"Okay..."

He nodded. "Good, good."

The clinic hadn't been open when they'd first arrived, but now it was full of coughing, sneezing, groaning patients who spilled out of the waiting room and into the main hallway. Jude charged ahead, eyes fixed on the doors, but Rain lagged behind. She could help these people, too, couldn't she?

"Jude." She pointed at the crowd.

He turned toward her, confused. It took a moment for it to dawn

77

on him what she was proposing, and when it did, he shook his head. "Sparingly," he said, making no sense.

Rain would have gone in anyway if he hadn't looked so... haunted. Jude bolted from the hospital with Rain struggling to follow.

CHAPTER EIGHT

RAIN FELT AS THOUGH SOMEONE had poked a hole in the top of her head, deflating her. By the time they'd reached the parking lot, her limbs were rubber, breathing became a chore, and she just wanted to rest. The high that had accompanied Keith's healing was gone.

Jude seemed too engrossed in his own thoughts to notice. He parked, unlocked the doors, and waited. Rain summoned a deep-down strength to open the door and swung her feet onto the gravel. If she could just make it into the apartment...

The car was gone before she reached the stairwell.

Each step was debilitating. Maybe she'd caught leprosy after all. Did it take effect that fast? Rain shook her head. No. It was impossible. She was the Messiah, God dammit. Her grip on the handrail slipped, and her face skidded over the unforgiving carpet.

Oh, come on.

Relinquishing her dignity in exchange for safe passage through the hallway, Rain crawled.

Finally in front of her door, she looked up and cursed the doorknob for being so fucking high. Who the hell designed doors this way, anyway? Idiots.

Rain whacked the door with the palm of her hand. "Francine?" It came out little more than a whisper, but it was enough to push her over the edge. She couldn't fight the weight on her eyelids anymore.

She raised her hand to hit the door one more time and passed out before her hand made contact.

In that realm between asleep and awake, Rain heard voices arguing in hushed, hurried tones. She couldn't tell the genders of the voices, only that they were getting louder, and she wanted them to shut up so she could go back so sleep. It'd been the deepest, most dreamless sleep she'd ever experienced, and she didn't want it to end.

Something wet dripped behind her ear, and the delicious cocoon of sleep unraveled, layer by layer, until her eyes were open. Francine held a wet towel to Rain's forehead as she glared at Jude. Neither seemed to notice Rain's eyes on them.

"How could you even think that she was ready for something like that?" Francine said, attempting to whisper.

"That's the point, though, isn't it? She shouldn't have to be ready."

Francine scoffed.

"I think you're getting in over your head here, Francine." Jude drew out the syllables of her name sarcastically.

"Yeah? Well, so are you." She pointed to Rain with her free hand, and they both turned to look at her.

At the sight of Rain's open eyes, they went quiet. Francine grimaced. Jude cleared his throat.

"How are you feeling?" Francine knelt next to the couch. "You passed out."

"I didn't pass out. I fell asleep. There's a difference. I think."

She tried to sit up, but Francine pushed her back down. "No, no, no. Just rest. Go back to sleep."

Jude said nothing, but the muscles in his face loosened, and his jaw unclenched. He'd been worried.

Shortly after they left the room, Rain drifted back to sleep. She couldn't properly address the weirdness of what she'd heard without at least another twelve hours' worth.

Rain woke to the sound of her stomach growling. She tried to ignore it, but then her bladder joined the conspiracy to get her off the couch.

She ambled to the bathroom, clutching her gut. Just a few more steps. She'd barely gotten her pants down before involuntarily unclenching, and enough urine to fill a pool rushed from her body. Rain shivered with relief. She wiped and glanced up at the clock next to the mirror. According to it, she'd only been asleep two hours.

She frowned. As far as naps went, it wasn't epic, but it'd done the trick. Her muscles cooperated without protest, and her brain had cleared itself of the haze that came from being over-tired.

Now, food.

She almost never ate at home, so she was not surprised to find the contents of her fridge to be about a thousand bottles of salad dressing, leftovers from Maxwell's that smelled suspiciously like mold, a few apples, and half a carton of eggs. She settled for a package of freeze-dried Asian noodles.

As Rain put a pot of water on the stove to boil, Francine came through the front door in her work clothes.

"You're home early."

Francine jumped. "Oh, thank God, I thought you were never going to wake up."

"This coming from someone who sleeps until noon every day? I was out for two hours, tops."

"No, Rain. You came home yesterday. You slept for twenty-six hours."

Rain's stomach growled again. *Better make it two packages of noodles. And maybe an apple.* Rain felt eyes boring into her skull while she crushed the noodles against the counter. "Yes?"

"You seem weirdly okay with what I just told you."

"Considering the last couple of weeks, a bit of oversleeping seems almost normal." She stared at the pot, willing it to boil faster. Amazingly, it did. "I'm sure Jude told you all about what happened at the hospital." Rain turned to gauge Francine's reaction.

But Francine had already begun walking to the bedroom. "Yeah," she called back.

Yeah? That's all she has to say?

Rather than pursue the issue, Rain finished preparing her dinner and ate in silence at the counter. *More secrets, always more secrets.*

The worst part of it was that Francine seemed to think Rain was too stupid to know when Francine was keeping things from her. Once, Rain found out about an on-the-side lover, and it had turned her off of revealing the woman's secrets for good. No, she wouldn't pry because if she did, it would only hurt.

That night, Francine suggested going out for a drink. They hadn't spoken since she came home from work, and Rain suspected it was her way of forcing them into conversation. Reluctantly, Rain agreed.

Thanks to Jude's envelopes of cash, Rain was no longer confined to manipulating Joey into free drinks at Maxwell's. Instead, they decided on a gay bar just outside the city: the Loft, oldest gay bar in the city, which boasted the city's oldest clientele. It was quiet, the drinks were heavy-handed, and she wouldn't have to watch Francine squirm in her seat every time a nice body walked by. It was perfect.

Rain chose a seat at the far end of the bar and waited for the bartender—affectionately called Minnie because of her black hair and big ears—to notice. Francine made a beeline for the bathroom.

"What can I get you, sweetie?" Minnie said.

Rain opened her mouth, and Jude's voice filled the void. "She'll have a coke."

Minnie raised her eyebrow.

"Jack and Coke, please." Rain turned to Jude. "Do I even want to know how you found me?"

"I'm your agent. I know everything." He slid into the stool on her left and slapped a rolled-up newspaper on the bar. His spooked aura from the day before seemed to have subsided, but his resolve also seemed to have weakened, like a person who saw danger ahead but had accepted its inevitability.

Minnie brought her drink, and Rain slipped her a card, mouthing *tab*.

Jude sighed. "You're going to need to curb the drinking."

"Why's that?"

He unrolled the paper and flipped to the second page. "Because

Mister Former Editor works fast. I was hoping for a front page story but..." He shrugged.

Rain squinted over the paper. The bar light was almost impossible to read in. At the center of the page, a headline read, "Former Editor of the Tribune Miraculously Healed."

She looked up at Jude.

"Keep reading."

She skimmed the article until she found her name—just Rain— and read the quote:

> *Of course I was skeptical at first, but just look at me. Rain— she called herself the Messiah—touched me, and instantly, I was healed. My sister and daughter will testify to this. My crackpot doctors sat around with their thumbs up their asses for weeks, and this woman took it all away in a second. It was a miracle. An honest to God miracle.*

"This is good though. Isn't it?"

"It's fantastic. But it means you're going to be getting a lot more attention soon, and you need to clean up your image. Otherwise, people will not take you seriously."

Rain shook the paper. "*Miracle*, Jude. I don't think people will care."

"Oh, they'll care. Why do you think Jesus was crucified? People followed and believed in him, but the way he behaved made people uneasy. Even his hair was an issue."

"His hair?"

"Pick up a history book. The Romans occupied the area two thousand years ago and were crazy about conformity. People groomed themselves to look like them: short hair, shaved beard. Jesus wore his hair like the rebels, which didn't win him any points once the Jews turned on him." He ran his fingers through his own thinning mop. "People are terrified of what's different. No one knows that better than someone like you. That's what makes you so... right." Jude glanced up at the ceiling and smirked, shaking his head.

Rain gulped her drink. Crucifixion over a haircut? The worst part wasn't even the fact that it was believable. People had been beaten in the streets for less. The worst part was that those kinds of thoughts made her feel as though she were constantly balancing the tight rope between confidence in her position as the Messiah and complete and utter despair. How could she be sure that she was right for it? In a matter of weeks, her entire belief system, or lack thereof, had been turned on its head. Rain could perform a thousand miracles, and she still wouldn't feel up to the task.

Francine returned from the bathroom with her hair tied up and a thicker layer of makeup on her face. She sat next to Jude. Rain's insides stirred.

"Rain has the night off," she said pointedly and winked at Rain.

Jude rolled his eyes. "I was just here to show her this." He dropped the paper in Francine's lap and stood. He turned to Rain. "We can let word of mouth do its thing for a few days. Just stay out of trouble. We don't want to ruin what we've started."

When Jude was out of earshot, Francine scoffed. "We, we, we. Fucking pompous—"

"What's the deal with you and Jude?" Rain said. She'd finished her drink, dislodging the rock she kept her suspicions buried under. "I could swear you know jack shit about each other, but there's something... *between* you two."

Francine forced a laugh. "I don't know what you mean."

"Are you fucking him?" Rain regretted it the instant the question left her lips, but she let it hang there like a red cloak in front of a bull.

"You're crazy."

"Maybe. Maybe I am. But you know what? You would be too if I hid everything from you the way you do with me. What am I supposed to think?"

"Problem, ladies?" Minnie planted her hands on the bar.

"No. There's no problem." Francine stood.

Rain felt Francine's glare but refused to meet her eyes. Her retreating footsteps fell like tiny axes on Rain's heart.

"Another drink, hon?" Minnie said.

Rain nodded. The smart thing to do was to pour gasoline on a fire, right?

At the opposite end of the bar, a woman with dark hair tied

back in a thick ponytail stared. Rain raised her glass. The woman continued to stare without blinking. It was probably the whiskey, but she thought she saw the woman's eyes sink into her head, leaving black holes in her face.

Minnie cut Rain off after her fourth drink. It was just as well because Rain wouldn't have been able to see her fifth clearly enough to grip it. She signed her credit slip, *Messiah*, and wobbled into the parking lot.

This wasn't the first time Francine had left her stranded at a bar. In fact, it seemed to be her favorite form of punishment when Rain fucked up. And for someone who wasn't technically in an exclusive relationship, Rain seemed to fuck up a lot. Was it her fault that she loved Francine? No. It was Francine's fault. Yeah. Maybe this whole Messiah thing was a blessing. She could focus on it instead of Francine. She could love the world instead of Francine. She could let her feelings for the bitch pool around the base of her chest and leak, drop by drop, until they were flushed from her system.

Without Rain's permission, tears welled up and spilled down her face.

CHAPTER NINE

BELIAL HAD NEVER LAID EYES on his mistress, a fact that was the subject of relentless taunting from the others in his horde. While they made preparations to go above—training, molding armor out of the brimstone and silver mines near the fifth circle, and polishing the bones of the dead for weapons—Belial could usually be found mucking out the shit pit of his mistress's pet, Garmr.

Usually, but not today.

Today, Belial had been chosen to personally deliver a message to his mistress. It didn't matter that there was no one else around to do it. In his mind, opportunity had finally smiled on the poor, shit-mucking demon.

There was no paper in Hell. All the fire made it impractical. So all messages had to be conveyed verbally. Belial stood behind the massive doors leading to his mistress's war rooms, repeating the message under his breath so as not to forget it while he waited to be summoned. This was his chance to make a name for himself, and he would not fuck it up.

The doors split, and an imp with a cat-like face ushered Belial inside.

A long metal table covered with maps took up most of the room. Wax figures were strewn over the maps. One of them looked vaguely similar to Belial's direct supervisor, Azazel. The figure's leg had been gnawed to a splinter.

Belial snickered.

"Something funny, worm?"

He froze. There was no mistaking the voice. It was her. But where was it coming from? As far as Belial knew, he was alone...

"I asked you a question." Her voice echoed through the room.

"N-n-no, Mistress. Nothing." He suddenly had no idea what to do with his claws. Crossing them would be deemed an offense, and he couldn't just let them hang there. Maybe if he held them behind his back or—

"Quit squirming, and deliver your message."

Belial nodded, but when he opened his mouth, nothing came out. He'd forgotten the message.

Her disappointed sigh sent shivers down his back. He'd be thrown into the tar pits for this. Or worse.

"Fuck it. We'll write on the skin of worthless minions like this lump. I've had enough. Do you see, imp? This is exactly why we've never been able to infiltrate the earth. Because of idiots like—"

"Mistress?" Belial faced a flogging for interrupting her, but he'd only just remembered. "The message is: Girl located. Arranging for pick up."

The Mistress released a moan of pleasure. "Good," she muttered. "Good."

The imp appeared from behind a tapestry depicting the early days of the war when his mistress had been at the height of her power and escorted Belial out of the war rooms.

Belial breathed in the sulfuric air, and for a moment, it didn't bother him. He'd been in the presence of the Mistress. Sure, he hadn't *actually* seen her, but he could always lie.

The next two nights, Rain slept on the couch, hoping to catch Francine just as she walked in the door. Even if she planned to let her go, Rain still wanted to apologize. Lovers or not, when Francine disappeared, there was always a chance she might not come back at all. Rain used to think Francine was worth the worry. Now, she just wanted to bury it all: the feeling, the constant uncertainty over where she stood in Francine's eyes.

On the fourth morning, Rain woke to the sound of voices outside her front window. At first, they were quiet, but as the morning progressed, they became louder and more restless. Aching from another night on the couch, she trudged, hunched over and clutching her lower back, to the window. She peeked through the blinds.

A crowd of people stood clumped together on the moat of grass that surrounded the apartment building, spilling out into the parking lot. One of the other tenants honked at a group huddled directly behind his car. Most of the people were middle-aged, a few younger, and fewer still were well into their eighties. A woman dressed in terrifyingly pink scrubs stood behind a wheelchair-bound child, clutching a red umbrella against the sun. The glow on the child's gaunt face looked demonic. A frail-looking man stood next to them, holding a sign that read, "Heal Her."

Rain didn't have time to wonder how they'd found her. One face stood out against the fringes of the crowd, lips pursed and forehead crinkled in disgust. Detective Park.

Rain's chest tightened. *Fuck.*

Had there been another bombing in the name of Messiah? Or was she just here to find a reason to arrest her? Rain wasn't going to stick around to find out.

She dressed and then tore her room apart looking for her wallet and keys, only to discover they were already in her pocket. She couldn't get to her car without being noticed. Even if the people in the crowd didn't know what Rain looked like—and she couldn't imagine how they would—Detective Park did and would no doubt draw attention to Rain the moment she was spotted. Rain would have to slip out the back security door and walk… somewhere. She cursed Francine for not being there to help and Jude for whatever part he'd played in the chaos outside because she knew—she *knew*—he'd had something to do with it.

The security door led to a grassy area shared by another complex. The wall of the building stretched out far enough that, though the area was completely devoid of anything remotely resembling a hiding place, Rain was confident the crowd and Detective Park wouldn't spot her.

She ran, making a beeline through the grass to the road farthest from the building. If she could just hide out for a few hours, maybe they would all get bored of waiting and go home.

The road was busy with morning rush hour traffic. Rain turned, and a pair of men in black clothes and masks jumped from a black van. They ran with long, powerful strides. Her stomach dropped. It took an excruciating minute for her legs to obey her brain's command to get the fuck out of there. Rain could have had a ten-minute head start and it wouldn't have mattered. These guys were fast. Too fast. And in a second, they were on her. One clamped his gloved hand over her mouth while the other helped drag her to the van. She tried a desperate kick to the second guy's abdomen. He caught it, holding her leg up, her arms pinned behind her back against the first guy. She groped him, looking for something sensitive to pinch, but his clothes were too bulky. Tears welled in her eyes. She blinked them back. Panicking wouldn't help.

They dragged Rain into the backseat then tied her wrists and ankles together. In one smooth movement, the first guy's hand was off her mouth, replaced by a thick strip of duct tape. She felt the van lurch into traffic.

A disturbing thought lit up Rain's mind. With all that Messiah bullshit Jude spewed, it hadn't occurred to her until this moment that Jude could be the bomber, but now she could think of nothing else. Were these his men? His enemies? And where were they taking her? Rain tried to count seconds in her mind to figure out how far they were moving but abandoned the task when she realized it wouldn't matter if she didn't know the direction.

A phone rang. The man who'd duct-taped her mouth pulled a cell phone from his pocket and put it to his ear. "Got her." He hung up.

Rain's breath caught. His voice was familiar, but she couldn't place it. She searched her memory, desperately clinging to the way his voice rattled when he spoke, until she gave herself a headache.

Suddenly, the van stopped, and the driver cut the ignition.

One of the men blindfolded Rain with a strip of cloth and unbuckled her. She struggled to keep from crying or passing out.

89

Don't panic, she thought, *someone would have seen them take you. The road was busy. Just keep it together.*

Rain whimpered.

They carried her, breathing heavily in her ear. She heard a door open, and the skunky stench of pot hit her like a wall. They set her on a cushion, probably a couch, and a burp of dust flew up her nose. The material of the couch scratched the bit of skin on her back where her shirt had ridden up.

Rain strained her ears for the sound of sirens. *Any minute now*, she thought, not believing it.

Soft footsteps approached her. She felt a tug at the back of her head where the blindfold had been tied and braced herself. Her captors were going to show her their faces, which, according to every cop show ever, meant they probably planned to kill her. Her stomach dropped as the blindfold was removed. She took in the image of the woman in front of her, and the fear rushed out of Rain's body, replaced by white-hot anger.

"Mmm?" *Fucking duct tape.*

Rain's mother stood over her, looking like G.I. Jane if G.I. Jane had been in Greenpeace rather than the military. Her hair had been buzzed off, and her cargo pants barely hung on her bony hips. Her face was thin, almost skeletal, as though she'd recently been on a hunger strike, which, Rain thought, wouldn't have been a stretch to assume.

She almost preferred the idea of an anonymous assassin.

After a quick glance over the living room, she wasn't surprised to recognize it as her childhood home. The furniture had all been taken out of the room except the couch she now sat on, but even it looked as though it'd been pulled out of storage at the last minute. The walls were covered in marked up maps and posters promoting a local animal rights organization and a few others Rain didn't recognize. What little wallpaper was visible was yellowed and peeling at the seams.

"It's unfortunate our reunion had to happen this way, Rainfall, but you didn't leave me much choice. And I'm sorry to say the ties and duct tape are going to have to stay on until you've calmed down. I can see the fire in your eyes, and I don't want you causing a fuss."

A fuss? A FUSS? The woman kidnaps me and worries that I might make a fuss? Rain hadn't thought her mother could fall deeper into insanity, yet here was the proof. She licked her lips, using as much saliva as she could to loosen the tape. She would not stay in this nuthouse a second longer than it took to escape.

"Are you thirsty? Just shake your head yes or no."

Rain nodded. She wasn't thirsty, but she wanted her mother out of the room. She could hop to the door and over to the neighbor's house. If they were the same couple who'd lived there when Rain was a kid, they would be all too pleased to have a reason to sic the cops on her parents. They were always coming over to "warn" her mother about her "behavior." The Department of Child Services had been mentioned on more than one occasion.

"I'll be right back," her mother said. "Oh, and don't try anything silly, okay? She pointed to the corner of the room where a video camera was pointed directly at the couch. "Daddy will see."

Her mother left the room, leaving Rain to stew with questions. This new level of crazy was scary, even for her mother.

She came back holding a cup of water Rain knew would've come from a bucket somewhere. When she was a kid, her parents had refused to use city water and instead waited for a good downpour to collect runoff for baths and cooking. During a drought, it wasn't unusual for Rain and her siblings to go days without bathing.

"I'm going to take the tape off your mouth now and untie your arms. Do you think you can be a good girl for Mommy and sit quietly?"

Mommy. The word was like a spider in Rain's ear, and she fought the convulsion it threatened. Rain knew she had to play along if there was going to be any chance of escape. She nodded.

"Good. I told your father this would be easy. You're not a bad girl. Just… misguided."

She looked into the blinking red light of the camera as her mother peeled the tape from her mouth, leaving her lips raw and tingly. Rain imagined her father looking away from his monitor. He'd always left the dirty work of discipline to his wife. No stomach for it. A plan began to form in Rain's mind.

She accepted the cup of water but didn't drink. Something brown and mucousy floated in it.

"If you wanted to talk to me," Rain said, lip curled. "You could have picked up a phone. Kidnapping, aside from being illegal, isn't necessary."

Her mother smiled. "Oh, honey, you and I both know that if we called, you wouldn't have picked up."

Rain shrugged. She had a point.

Her mother continued, "Besides, this type of thing needs to be done in person."

"What thing?"

"An intervention."

Rain opened her mouth, but no words came to her.

Her mother fetched a sheet of newspaper from beneath the couch and held it open for Rain to look at. It was the article Jude had shown her at the bar.

"Seriously? That's what this is about?" Rain laughed. She figured there would be a run-in with the religious crazies at some point. She just hadn't bargained on them being ones with whom she shared a few chromosomes.

"Not just this, sweetheart. I saw the report about the Dorothy Day center. I didn't make much of it then, but after reading this article, I could see what was happening. What you'd become. How could you renounce Mother Nature in the name of this... this..." She balled up the paper and threw it at Rain's face. "This filth! We taught you better than to accept these delusions as truth."

The newspaper fell into Rain's cup and slowly soaked up the putrid water. She put the cup on the ground and sighed. What was she supposed to do? Contradict the woman knowing full well that it would mean being trapped in this house for God knew how long, or play her game and risk her mother's Olympic-worthy rage fest? Her mother may have been slight, but the woman always found the strength to teach her children a lesson. Rain and her sister had been their mother's most frequent pupils. Denial wouldn't work, either. Her mother was as single-minded as she was vengeful. Avoidance was the only option.

"Where's Dad?"

Her mother frowned. "He's taking care of a few things."

"Can I see him?"

"You don't want to spend quality time with your mother?"

"I haven't seen him in years either," Rain said, sidestepping her mother's trap.

The frown softened. "You'll see him soon. We're all going to sit down and have a little chat. See if we can't wrench those disgusting little ideas out of your head."

A young woman—she couldn't have been older than twenty—squeaked in, wearing a dress that looked like a potato sack over tattered jeans. It took a minute for Rain to recognize her sister. Rain had been fifteen the last time she saw River, though they'd had occasional phone contact, the last of which had been on Rain's birthday a little over two years ago. At the time, River had sounded as if she was finally cutting the cord. Now, it looked as though her sister had been sucked right back into the Johnson crazy tide.

"It's good to see you, Rainfall." River threw her long black tresses over her shoulder. She was easily the more beautiful of the sisters and twice as compassionate. Snow White in burlap.

"You too," Rain said, meaning it.

To their mother, River said, "I'll sit with her. Dad needs some help downstairs."

Their mother sighed, retying the rope around Rain's hands. "Just in case."

When their mother was gone, River sat on the couch next to Rain and plumped the cushion behind her back. "I told her the rope wasn't necessary."

"So untie me."

"And face the wrath of Hurricane Emily?" River shook her head. "It'll be over in a couple of days. Just tell her what she wants to hear."

"A couple of days? Are you kidding me? River, come on. You can't seriously be okay with this." Rain presented her bound wrists to emphasize her point.

River stared into her lap, her lips pressed into a tight line.

Rain wanted to believe the indecision was because of her mother's manipulation. Rain had been gone for years, and there was no telling what lies their mother had spun in Rain's absence. But on River's face, she read a far more disturbing expression. Rain's sister didn't *want* to untie her.

When they were kids, Rain would have done anything for River. Her sister, Rain assumed, would have done the same. What had changed?

Rain bit her lip. "Do you remember when you were in fifth grade and you got to bring home the class guinea pig for the weekend?" *The hell was that thing's name?* "You loved Buttercup. Even made him a little hat out of a bottle cap."

The corner of River's mouth twitched. Her eyes remained dark.

"Mom had a fit. After she set Buttercup free in the backyard, she made you sleep in a makeshift cage for the night so you could see what it was like to be trapped."

Tears filled River's eyes. Rain's chest ached, but she had to remind her sister of what their mother had done. Would continue to do. "Who let you out when mom was asleep so that you could sleep in your bed? Who stayed up all night, listening for footsteps so you wouldn't get caught?"

River sniffled then looked up at Rain. "Okay." With shaking hands, she began to untie her wrists.

"Oh, River." Their mother stood in the doorway, arms crossed. "You too?"

Both women jumped. River's eyes widened, and Rain's heart sank. She couldn't let River take the brunt of their mother's anger. No matter what, Rain was still the big sister.

"I have to pee. River was going to take me to the bathroom."

Her mother looked to River for confirmation. Rain hoped that her sister's ability to lie had improved since childhood. River nodded.

"Fine," her mother said. "But make it fast. Your brother's almost here. Then we can get started."

Rain waited patiently for her sister's shaky fingers to finish untying the rope then allowed herself to be led to the back hallway. The doors to their childhood bedrooms were shut tight, and where simple brass doorknobs had been, industrial-sized deadbolts had taken their places. Rain shot her sister an inquisitive look, but River shook her head. Rain had lost whatever hold she'd had on River the moment their mother had come into the room. She would have to get out on her own.

The door to the bathroom hadn't been messed with, for which Rain was grateful. If she remembered correctly, there was a window—a small, nearly impossible to open window—in the wall next to the bathtub. River seemed to read her mind. Before Rain closed the door behind her, she squeezed Rain's hand.

"River..."

"I'll wait outside the door until you're done," River said, loud enough for an eavesdropping mother to hear, and closed the door.

Emily held River beneath her thumb like an ant. What good was being the Messiah if she couldn't even help her own sister? Rain promised herself that once she was clear of this insane asylum, she'd figure out a way to get River out too.

Rain pushed aside the shower curtain, and her stomach lurched. The window was there, but it'd been covered by plywood. It wouldn't be difficult to break through, but it'd make a hell of a lot of noise, and there'd be nothing River could do to stop their mother and her twin goons from breaking down the door just to hog-tie her again. She climbed into the tub and inspected the board. The nails were small and could probably be pried away without drawing anyone's attention. But what to pry them with?

The medicine cabinet housed only half a bottle of melatonin and a pair of rusted tweezers. Rain pocketed the tweezers, hoping she wouldn't need to stab anyone in the eye. The smell of mold rolled out of the cabinet under the sink as soon as the door was opened. Rain held her breath as she felt around, hitting a few boxes and the slimy pipes that ran into the wall. Behind the pipes, though, her hand found something soft and stringy. She peered inside and spotted something that pushed the thought of escape to the back of her mind.

A wig. An *orange* wig. An orange wig that looked almost identical to Rain's haircut.

Son of a bitch. It was her.

Rain snatched the wig from its foam stand and yanked open the bathroom door, startling River. When she saw what Rain clenched in her fist, the color fell from her face.

"Is this what I think it is?" Rain demanded.

River blinked.

"Never mind. Where is she?"

Her sister pointed down. The basement.

Rain stormed past her sister, clutching the wig so tight the synthetic strands dug into her skin. The stairwell to the basement was hidden by an old maroon sheet. In front of the sheet stood the thugs who'd kidnapped her. Anger rippled through Rain's body. Then they looked at her, and their eyes glowed in the same way the woman's had at the bar: orange, as if they were on fire. Her skin prickled as fear and loathing battled for control over her body.

The taller of the pair crossed his arms. His partner grinned. His teeth were rotted and sharp like a dog's.

"Let me through," Rain said in the strongest voice she could muster.

The second man frowned.

"I said let me through," Rain said again, louder.

The muscles beneath their shirts bulged, but the men inched aside, clenching their jaws. Faces scrunched, their legs seemed to move without their permission, jerking and twisting.

"The fuck..." one of them murmured.

Rain threw aside the sheet and ran down the stairs, her heart hammering against her chest. Demons in her childhood home. Why were they here, and more importantly, why the hell were they working for her mother? And why was her mother trying to frame her for murder?

CHAPTER TEN

THE BASEMENT WAS WASHED IN the glow of seven black and white monitors that displayed the activity in each room of the house, the front and back yards, and the roof. Bits of newspaper were strewn across the concrete floor. In the back corner, hovering over a table of wire, plastic bits, and a million other odds and ends, were Rain's parents. Her father fiddled with a wire stripper while her mother watched over his shoulder.

If Rain needed any further proof of the conclusion she'd drawn upon finding the wig, this was the smoking gun. Her mother was the eco-terrorist, Messiah. And she was doing it while wearing a wig that made her look just like her daughter.

"You bitch." Rain threw the wig onto the table.

Her father refused to look up.

Her mother sneered. "Don't speak to me that way. I'm your mother."

"You're a psychopath." *Or something worse.*

Sighing, her mother walked around the table, blocking Rain's view of her father. "You're confused, Rainfall. You've been away from me for so long that you've lost sight of what's important."

Rain shook her head. The woman was certifiable.

"That's why I brought you here, dear. You're been sucked into that… fiction… and acting on behalf of a group of people who'd rather see people dead than accept them as they are."

"Are you fucking listening to yourself? That's exactly what you're doing. Only you're actually killing people. *And*"—she pointed to the wig—"you're doing it as me! There's a detective watching my apartment because she thinks I'm a murderer!" And then it dawned on her. "That's why you sent those idiots to pick me up. You knew they were watching me. Knew they'd figure it out eventually. You wanted to make sure your little operation stayed hidden."

"To keep you safe, dear."

"Oh, please."

"You were drawing too much attention to yourself. Putting an ad in the paper with your address? Honestly, Rainfall, I thought you were smarter than that."

Rain stopped. "What ad?"

Her mother handed her a folded scrap of newspaper from her pocket.

An ad about the size and shape of a business card boasted her name as the woman who had healed the editor and her home address. Rain's face burned, and her mouth went dry. Jude. Where the hell did he get off thinking it was okay to tell the world where she lived? She'd kill him.

"So you see, we had no choice but to come get you. We missed you, anyway. Didn't we?" Her mother shot a look over her shoulder.

Her father muttered, "Yes."

Rain stuffed the ad into her pocket. "You can't keep me here."

"It's just for a little while, Rainfall. Don't be so dramatic."

"No."

"Just until you understand where we're coming from. We'll help you. All of us."

Rain bounced on the balls of her feet, ready to run.

"Darling, please…"

Fuck it. Rain turned and sprinted back up the stairs. The demons had disappeared, so nothing stood between her and escape. Without the time to consider that her clear route was intentional, she ran around the corner of the hallway, straight for the front door. Just as she reached out for the knob, rough hands gripped her waist from behind and dragged her backward.

"Get the fuck off of me!" She twisted and kicked, throwing her head back against the man's chest.

"Mom said you'd be difficult," the man's voice said before a needle pricked her arm.

Her legs crumpled beneath her. Darkness fell.

Before she opened her eyes, Rain knew she'd been tied up again. Rope scratched the soft part of her wrists and ankles. A cold, clammy hand rested on the inside of her calf. When she did finally open her eyes, Rain felt transported back to the day in third grade she'd broken her ankle trying to fly. Faces from her childhood—mother, father, brother, sister—all stared down at her, familiar but frightening.

Her mother sat at Rain's feet, stroking Rain's leg.

Her brother, Sycamore, stood with arms crossed over his broad chest. Like their mother and father, he'd decided that having hair on his head stood in the way of whatever insanity went on in this house.

River stood behind Sycamore, head down, folded over on herself like a mouse in the presence of a starving cat. "How's your head?" she squeaked.

Their mother's jaw tightened at the sound of River's voice.

Rain blinked away a few lingering dots at the corners of her vision and shrugged. "Still attached."

Her father chuckled softly.

"It's your own fault." Her mother dug her nails into Rain's leg. "There was no reason for the theatrics."

"Says the woman who had her son stick a needle into her daughter," Rain said.

"If you can't keep your sarcastic comments to yourself, you're going to force me to help you," her mother snapped.

"You're threatening me?"

River took a step forward. "Mom, I don't think—"

"You've done quite enough thinking, dear. You're as much to blame for that bump on her head as she is."

River stepped back again, wounded. "Sycamore's the one who dropped her," she murmured.

God, would that girl ever grow a backbone? Rain had done everything she could when they were young to put herself between her sister and their mother when their mother's wrath was the worst, but now? River was an adult, for fuck's sake.

Rain sighed. "This has nothing to do with River. This is between you and me." Big sister to the rescue. "I'll cooperate with you."

Her mother smiled. "I'm very happy to hear that, Rainfall." She turned to Sycamore. "Run down to the basement, and get the kit." Then she stood and wrapped her arm around her husband's waist. "We knew you'd come around."

Rain couldn't help noticing her father turn a faint shade of green.

Sycamore returned carrying a large, fraying carpetbag with brass handles. He sat it on the ground, and her mother knelt to rifle through it, pulling out an egg, a sheet of ragged black silk, a pink stone tied with rainbow-colored yarn, what looked like a pigeon feather, and a box of incense.

"Lovely," her mother said. "This will be a fantastic cleansing, I think."

"You're exorcising me."

"No, no, no," Sycamore said. "That's something those *pretenders* do."

Her mother laughed.

Sycamore continued, "This will cleanse your aura and wash away the negativity and false thoughts they've brainwashed you into believing."

"Takes one to know one," Rain said.

Her mother clicked her teeth. "Enough." She handed River the box of incense and raised her eyebrow as if to say, *"Do you think you can handle this without fucking up?"*

River lit each stick with a cigarette lighter and placed them in ceramic bowls that'd been placed around the perimeter of the room.

A throbbing pain began in the back of Rain's head and radiated around her skull before settling right behind her eyes. *What the hell did they give me?*

"Shall we start with the egg?" her mother said.

Sycamore nodded, River averted her eyes, and her father looked ready to throw up.

"And what exactly do you plan to do with that?"

Her mother opened her mouth but was interrupted by her father. "Before we start"—he swallowed hard—"I'd like to have a word in private with my daughter."

Her mother raised an eyebrow.

"We don't know how long this process will take or whether she'll be conscious at the end of it. I want to speak to her while I have a moment to do so. You had your time."

Rain tried to read his face, but he refused to look at her.

"Fine," her mother said. "We'll all wait downstairs."

"No. I'll take her downstairs." He nodded to the door. "We don't want another accident."

Her mother nodded. "Yes, I think that's best. I'll finish setting up here. Sycamore, River." She handed them the items from the bag.

Rain's father scooped her up as if she were five again and carried her from the couch, through the house, and back downstairs to the basement. She didn't know whether to be scared or relieved.

He sat her on the chair behind the desk then disappeared back upstairs. Rain heard a door shut.

"Security door," he said as he descended the stairs once again. "For emergencies."

"What kind of emergencies?"

"Technically, it's to hide us in the event that we're found out. Personally, I think this is more of an emergency."

"I'm confused."

"Story of my life."

He produced a Swiss army knife from his back pocket and knelt next to the chair. With a few quick cuts, the rope fell from her wrists and ankles. Rain allowed herself a moment to breathe, to revisit the possibility of escape. Then she remembered the hold her mother had over her family even when she wasn't looking.

"Is this is a trick?"

He placed the knife in her lap. "No. I'm getting you out of here. Behind the monitors is a window. It's small, but you'll probably fit."

Rain stood, clutching the knife, ignoring the pounding in her head. It'd gotten worse. She hoped she didn't have a concussion.

Her father grabbed her arm, and Rain's breath caught. "But before you go, I really would like to talk to you."

Rain groaned.

"No. I mean, yes, I want to talk to you but not the way you think." He gestured to the chair. "Please."

She sat, feeling safer for having a weapon, though she'd never be able to use it against her father. Rain glanced up at the window once before looking back at him. Lines cut like caverns into his forehead, and his cheeks were hollow. He looked *old*. "Okay. What do you want to talk about?"

Stuffing his hands in his pockets, he said, "How've you been these last..."

"Five years? Cut the platitudes, Dad, and get to the point. I didn't see you stepping in front of Sycamore before he jammed a needle full of God knows what into me."

"Okay. Fine. Fair enough. I was wondering..." He paused. "Do you really believe that you're the Messiah?"

Rain hesitated, thinking it might be a loaded question, but there was something in her father's expression that made her think otherwise, nothing like the judgment she saw in her mother. "Yes."

"Was that real? What we read about in the paper?"

"Yes."

"Good. That's... that's good, right? Yes. Good." He exhaled slowly, rubbing his face. Rain imagined she could see the cogs turning in his mind, crunching and pounding the realization into something more palatable. "So what now?"

Accepted? Just like that?

"Now I leave through that little window, and you stall long enough for me to get to a phone."

"You're planning to call the cops then."

"I... don't know." There was no doubt in Rain's mind that her mother should be behind bars. It was obvious she wasn't going to stop the bombings. As for her siblings and father... the jury was still out. Her mother was manipulative, conniving, and cruel when she needed to be. Who knew if they'd have even considered the bombings if it hadn't been for her? Rain *would* get the Detective involved, if for no other reason than to clear her own name. Just not yet.

Her father moved to embrace her then reconsidered and awkwardly patted her back. "Be careful."

Rain snorted. "You be careful."

He smiled, but it didn't touch his eyes.

"Right then." He strode across the basement to the window.

It took some calculated shoving, but the window finally fell open. He lifted Rain by her waist—something he hadn't done since she was little—and helped her wriggle through the small opening. The ancient metal frame scraped down her sides, catching on her belt. Her father grabbed her calves and shoved, and she was through with minimal scrapes and bruising. She wondered if she'd need a tetanus shot.

The road was empty, and fortunately, no one waited at the front door. The sun, half-hidden behind a copse of trees at the end of the block, cast pink and yellow rays over them like a crown. She'd been trapped in the house all day. Her stomach growled.

Rain turned to take one last look at the window to see her father staring and waving limply.

She leaned down so that her voice wouldn't carry over the yard. "What was the egg for, anyway?"

Her father blinked. "Some people, like your mother, believe that placing a hen's egg in the... erm... vagina will draw out negativity."

"Seriously?"

"Get out of here." He backed away. Faint footsteps echoed down into the basement. "I'll take care of it."

"Thanks, Dad."

Rain turned and ran without looking back.

Her parents' house was miles from her apartment. Part of her knew that going home wasn't smart—her mother knew where she lived—but the need to be somewhere familiar won out.

Rain's legs burned from disuse. She could have called a cab from the corner store, but she had spent the better part of the last week either on her couch or tied up. Her muscles needed to work.

Once a safe distance from the house and fairly certain she wasn't being followed, the fear Rain had swallowed around her mother reared its ugly head, making her wary of anything that might surround or trap her. She walked in the middle of the road, anxious to keep as much open space around her as possible.

Rubbing her wrists where the rope had all but broken the skin, it occurred to her that she probably could have gotten out much sooner. If Rain could cure necrotizing fasciitis, what had stopped her from untying a little bit of rope? She supposed that if she had, the wig wouldn't have been found. Maybe she was meant to suffer a little for the sake of figuring it out. Or maybe it'd just been the presence of her mother, reducing her to the pre-teen and teenage years, all defiance and anger without practical thought. Hellish years for all of the Johnson kids.

There had to be a way to get River out of that house. Sycamore was a lost cause. He was the oldest and, being the only son, had the most to prove. Not that it was asking much of him to instigate chaos and damage. As a kid, her brother had found joy in pitting Rain and River against each other by destroying their toys and claiming to have seen the other do it. It was ironic how Rain looked the most like their mother but possessed little to none of her other qualities.

The stars had long come out by the time Rain reached her apartment building. The crowd had gone, but their trash remained: abandoned signs hastily written on cardboard, fast food bags and napkins, Styrofoam coffee cups. Would it have killed them to walk the hundred feet to the dumpster? Her legs ached, and her stomach begged for something, anything to fill it, but she couldn't bring herself to ignore the filth. She trudged upstairs, retrieved a garbage bag from beneath the kitchen sink, and began cleaning up their mess.

PART TWO

"You can have peace, or you can have freedom.
Don't ever count on having both at once."

-Robert A. Heinlein

CHAPTER ELEVEN

JUDAS HAD SEEN THE VAN. Instinct drew his attention to the wafts of smoke pouring from the windows, smoke he was sure no one else would have been able to see. It all happened so fast.

Fueled by panic, he chased the van for as long as his ancient legs would move. This hadn't been part of the plan as Judas knew it. It wasn't until the van was out of sight that G had mumbled reassurances in his head.

It'll be good for her.

"I'm sure I don't have to ask if you know what was in that van with her."

Obviously.

"Then on what plane of existence will it be good for her? They'll devour her."

No. They won't.

Judas ignored Him after that. Judas didn't know where Rain was or *what* she was for that matter. That trick in the car tingled in the back of his brain. The healing, too. Francine had been right. Rain shouldn't have had to be prepared for anything so strenuous because she shouldn't have been able to do it in the first place. Judas was being played for a fool. He would have no part in this kidnapping fiasco. Let Him sort it out.

Judas sat up that night in his room at the Motel 6, head pounding from the safety-orange décor assaulting his eyes from every corner. Even with the lights off, the curtains and bedspread seemed to glow. He leaned back against the flattened pillows. Ancient cigarette smoke drifted up from beneath the pillowcase. He sighed and closed his eyes.

A sharp pain in his ribcage jolted Judas awake. He clutched his now hot side and squinted into the darkness for the culprit. He couldn't see her, but he could smell her. The stench was like rancid fruit and Baby Soft perfume, powdery and sickly sweet. She'd done a decent job of covering up the rotten-egg stink of sulfur, but Judas wasn't fooled.

Breathing deeply to calm his hammering heart, Judas groped the bedside table until he found the lamp and switched on the light.

"Lucifer," he said.

She sat cross-legged at the foot of the bed, long limbs draped in what looked like red silk at first glance. As he continued to take in the image of her, he noticed that the silk moved on its own, tightening around her slender body like a second skin. Her white hair was pulled back and tied intricately, making the lack of eyelashes and eyebrows on her face that much more disconcerting. On her hands, she wore rings that extended well past her fingertips and ended in knife-like points.

Judas's side throbbed.

"We're old friends, Judas. Call me Lucy." She licked her lips with a blood-red tongue. "It's been a long time."

"Has it? I haven't counted."

"Liar."

"Devil."

She clapped her hands. "Oh, I've missed this."

Judas shook his head.

"Don't be like that, dear."

"What do you want, Lucy?"

"To catch up, of course. It's been so long since we've talked, and I've missed our chats. You can't imagine how hard it is for me to find someone to talk to. All the cowering and stuttering..." She threw her hands up. "It's so... frustrating."

"Well, I'm all talked out. In case you haven't noticed, I've been plopped back into the land of the living, and the living need sleep. So if you don't mind." Judas made a show of stretching and yawning before leaning back against the headboard.

Quick as lightning, Lucy hovered over him, eyes ablaze. A hand jutted from beneath the silk—a third hand—and gripped Judas's face. The knotted fingers burned his cheeks, and he smelled cooking flesh.

"I'm doing you a favor, Judas Iscariot, so it'd behoove you to listen."

Tears stung his eyes. *Bitch.*

"Let go of my face," he said, his voice low and steady.

She snarled but relinquished her grip. Shadows darkened her eyes as she sat once again at the foot of the bed.

Judas stood and went to the bathroom where he wet a towel with cool water. He sat across from Lucy in the rickety desk chair and dabbed at his burns. Blood spotted the towel.

"Fine. I'm listening."

Lucy grinned. A fang poked over her lip. "Do you remember how we met, Judas?"

Like G, Lucy wasn't one to get right to the point of things. It was maddening, but if he wanted to leave the conversation intact, Judas would have to humor her.

"How could I forget?"

"Mmm." She nodded. "So skittish back then."

"I'll task you to find someone not skittish around a fire-breathing hydra woman-thing."

Lucy raised her eyebrow.

The burns stung. He'd forgotten what it was like to feel real physical pain. He hadn't missed it.

"True," she relented. "Lately I've opted for more subtle tactics."

Skin dress. Yeah. Real subtle.

"Are we going to wax poetic about the many faces of Lucy all night?"

"You really aren't fun anymore."

"I left my funny bone back in my grave."

Lucy hissed through clenched teeth. Flames licked her fingertips.

Judas leaned back in the chair, unblinking. Her moods were unpredictable, to say the least. One minute, Lucy would revel in witty banter. The next, she'd bite your head off for the same. Literally. Judas had witnessed one such event. The crunching sound of teeth through skull had haunted his nightmares for weeks afterward.

Lucy stood, the silk skin tightening around her womanly body as she stalked toward Judas. She stood behind him and encircled his neck in her arms. Heat radiated from her skin, burning like direct sunlight at the height of summer. Her scaly lips brushed his ear. Breath like the salty scent of female sex wafted over him.

"I want to help you," she whispered.

"How could you possibly help me?" Judas was keenly aware of her tightening grip.

"I know why you're here."

"Oh?" The fact didn't entirely surprise him.

"In fact, I knew before you knew."

"That's impossible."

"Hardly, pet." She loosened her hold on his neck but kept her hands on his shoulders, pinching them. "You and I know better than anyone that He has a way of... twisting things to suit His ends."

"And?"

"This time," she smiled and pressed her lips against Judas's stinging cheek, "I have the advantage."

"What advantage?"

"Knowledge."

"What knowledge?"

"Prior. As I said, I knew before you knew."

"Knew what?"

"His plan, you idiot." Lucy scratched a nail down the length of Judas's sleeve, splitting the fabric.

"It was my plan," he countered weakly.

She laughed. "No. It wasn't."

Might as well have been. He'd allowed himself to be dragged into it, offered himself and Rain like sacrificial lambs. "Fine. But how does knowing that help me?"

"I came up with my own plan, pet. Though, I admit I wasn't entirely ready for this. So many more souls on the brink of corruption." She looked longingly downward. "Still, I'm proud of my solution. The symmetry... it's perfect."

Judas turned his head and looked pointedly at Lucy for the first time since she'd invaded his room. "The Antichrist."

Lucy nodded, grinning rows of sharp, white teeth. "I'm telling you this because I feel an odd compulsion to give you a fighting chance, though we both know which side of the coin you'll land on when it all ends."

"Where is he?"

"*She* is in a safe place. Has been for quite some time."

His mouth went dry, tongue glued to the roof of his mouth.

Lucy licked the inside of Judas's ear. "Don't worry, pet. It'll all be over soon."

"How soon?"

She shook her head. "Don't spoil the fun for me."

With a snap of her fingers, the lamplight extinguished, and a rush of hot air pulled from the room like it was sucked through a vacuum.

Judas sat in the dark, a cold sweat dotting his brow. He waited for G's voice to boom through his mind, telling him that what Lucifer had claimed was a lie. The silence spoke volumes.

But Rain was just a girl. How could she be expected to do battle with the armies of Hell? It was impossible. So impossible that Judas felt himself pulled into doubting the Devil's claims. G wouldn't allow it. Would He?

Yes, Judas thought. *He would.*

Judas settled back into bed with the towel covering his face. At first light, Judas would go to Rain, and he would test her. If the antichrist was on Earth, Rain would show herself to be the Messiah. And if she was, then God help them all.

Gabriel picked at one of his feathers, plucked as penance for ungrateful thoughts. Behind him, Michael and Raphael measured vials of Glory and Redemption to pack with a skin of Hallelujah Chorus. All other activities had been suspended for official preparations.

"If you don't cut out that sulking, I'll pluck you naked," Michael said.

"It's only a sword," Raphael added. "Even if it was the most beautiful thing I'd ever set eyes on."

Michael elbowed him.

"Sorry."

"Listen, Gabe, why don't you head up to the armory? They'll get you a suitable replacement. Can't have you headed into battle empty-handed, eh?" Michael said.

Gabriel nodded. "Yeah. Okay."

The armory was located on the fifth floor of the main Trinity building, just above the executive offices. Too depressed to fly, Gabriel took the stairs. On the fourth floor, he heard voices.

Technically, no one was supposed to be outside of their assigned block during preparation hour. Curiosity got the better of him, and instead of continuing up the last flight of stairs, Gabriel sneaked along the wall toward the source of the voices.

Two men were arguing. One of the voices he recognized immediately as G.

"You said it wouldn't get this far."

"I said there wouldn't be a fight."

"The entire chorus of the Archangels and Seraphim are gathering weapons as we speak! They've been prepping since our meeting with Judas."

"Joshua, you're my son, so I'll ignore your doubt. Have faith."

"In what?"

"In the Great Plan."

Silence.

"Think we should invite the archangel in, Joshua? He seems very intrigued by the conversation."

Caught. Gabriel's head drooped. He'd never get the sword back now.

CHAPTER TWELVE

BY THREE A.M., RAIN MANAGED to clear most of the crowd's trash from the parking lot. She left the used condoms for the complex's maintenance staff. Even a Messiah had limits. She showered the stink of garbage and incense away then settled into bed, her arms too weak to pull on a shirt. For an hour, Rain stared at the ceiling. Her body felt dead, but her mind would not allow it sleep. She couldn't stop thinking about her sister and father, wondered what she was going to do about her mother... Wished that they were the only people she needed to worry about.

Rain hadn't changed because people never really changed, but her perspective had shifted. The people who'd gathered outside her apartment blindly followed the testimony of one man and an advertisement that anyone with thirty dollars could have submitted. People really were that desperate for hope, or at least for someone who would tell them hope was possible.

She still didn't think she was qualified for the job, but that didn't matter now. She'd seen demons in her childhood home, real ones, not conjured in her memories. Jude was wrong. There *was* something happening, and somehow her family had gotten involved. For River's sake, Rain had to at least try to be a savior.

Her eyes finally closed just as dawn broke, and she slid into a dreamless sleep.

In the interest of time, Judas wanted to skip the shower, but he could smell himself. Ripe. He washed gently, fearing scrubbing might cause his ancient skin to slough off. His fingertips had turned dark, as if he'd been finger painting with coal dust.

G still wasn't speaking to him, and Judas couldn't decide whether it was a blessing or an omen.

Rain's car sat in the parking lot in front of her apartment building. A good sign. After she was released, Judas had assumed Rain would get the hell out of Dodge. He would have.

Judas knocked three times before letting himself in. The kitchen was a mess: dishes piled and molding in the sink, an overflowing garbage bin. He guessed the rest of the apartment wasn't much better. Something was wrong.

Judas peered around the slightly ajar bedroom door and saw the orange spatter of her hair against the pillow. Still sleeping. Judas approached the room and immediately regretted it.

Rain lay naked and splay-legged on top of the covers, her chest rising and falling with each delicate snore.

His heart seized, and his groin hummed to life, only to shudder to a halt. He was getting too old for this. In an attempt to reduce the awkwardness that would surely take over the room once Rain woke, Judas tossed a small blanket from the floor over her body.

He studied her face. Asleep, she looked almost pleasant. She looked human. Too human. He didn't see the glow of the holiest of holies in her skin as he'd seen in Joshua the first time they'd met. There was no stirring of Judas's soul as he gazed upon her. Maybe it was just him. He'd seen too much, knew too much, and believed in none of it. Or maybe Lucy had been fucking with him. The Devil got bored just like anyone, and though he hated to admit it, Judas was an easy target.

"Rain."

No response.

"*Rain.*"

She snored.

Judas gently shook her shoulder, careful to avoid direct contact with her skin. It felt wrong to touch any part of her naked body, not out of concern for her modesty, but out of revulsion. Like walking in on a sibling and their lover and being offered a hug after.

Rain still didn't wake.

"Fine." Judas grabbed the pillow beneath her head and yanked.

Nothing. The end of the world was coming, and this girl would probably sleep through it. With the grace of a minor league baseball player, Judas swung the pillow in a wide arc and bashed Rain directly in the face.

She woke up flailing and elbowed Judas in the side bearing Lucy's love stab. Pain lit through him, but the look on her face alone was worth it.

"Jude?" she yelled. "What the fuck is wrong with you?"

"A lot. Get dressed."

Rain looked down, and her face reddened. "Get out."

He saluted and left the bedroom, closing the door behind him.

The part that troubled Rain wasn't the fact that Jude had walked into her apartment while she slept and smacked her with a pillow. It was that she wouldn't have covered herself with the scratchiest blanket she owned before falling asleep. Jude had seen her naked.

She dressed and emerged from the bedroom to find Jude digging through the pile of mail on her counter. He looked up, and she crossed her arms over her chest. He could see her tits through her sweater. She could feel it.

Rain raised an eyebrow. "Where have you been?"

"Around."

"Around?"

"Yes."

"Right."

Jude opened his mouth to say more but quickly closed it and turned his attention to the ceiling.

"What?"

"Nothing. I just—are you okay?"

"You knew where I was, didn't you?"

"Yes. Well, no. I saw the van."

Rain strode toward him, ready to throttle him. "You motherfucker."

He put his hands up. "Look, there was nothing I could do, okay? I had orders."

"Orders?"

"Kind of."

Rain shook her head. "Whatever. It doesn't matter. I don't think my mother would have hurt me anyway. At least, not permanently."

Did she really believe that? There'd been something more than disappointment in the way her mother had looked at her. Disgust. Wrath. Maybe even hatred.

"What happened to your face?"

Jude's hand flew up to the scabbed wounds on his cheek. He touched them gently with a fingertip and winced. "Accident."

"Like a tango with a soldering iron?"

He waved away her comment. "We'd better get moving."

"Another publicity miracle?"

"No."

Rain didn't push for an elaboration as she followed him out the door. She'd figure it out eventually when he shoved her into yet another uncomfortable situation.

"Are there any lakes around here?" he said once they were both in his car.

"Why?"

"Doesn't have to be a lake. A pond. Small river. A large fucking puddle."

Rain thought. "I'm pretty sure there's a lake behind the YMCA. Might be a pond."

"Good enough."

"Should I be worried?"

Jude laughed, wide-eyed and maniacal.

Patches of dry, dead grass surrounded a pond about as wide as a small parking lot. Rain couldn't tell how deep it was. Murky water obscured the view to the bottom. Without putting her fingers in, she knew the water would be freezing. Though the ice had thawed within the last month, the sun was never out long enough to warm the ground.

"Shit," Jude murmured, staring across the pond.

A group of four people dressed in robes and coats huddled close together, sipping from Styrofoam cups of steaming liquid.

"What's the problem?"

"I'd have preferred we were alone for this."

Jude seemed off. Half-joking, Rain said, "Drowning me won't work. I can swim."

He sighed. "You really are an idiot, aren't you?"

"Fuck off."

Jude glared. "Rain, I'm not going to be the one who tries to kill you." He held out his hand. "Give me your jacket, shoes, and socks."

I'm not going to be the one... Who was? "What are you talking about?"

"If this doesn't work, you'll want dry socks. Water's nippy."

"If what doesn't—oh." He wanted her to walk on water.

"C'mon. Off with the clothes."

"Why wouldn't it work?"

Jude shrugged.

"Anyone ever tell you you're the most unhelpful person ever?"

"Once. Let's get this over with."

Grudgingly, Rain removed her jacket, shoes, socks, and sweater, leaving her with her jeans and a painfully thin undershirt to guard against the wind as she walked. Or plunged. She inched toward the water lapping gently against the shore. The wind picked up. Water rippled over her bare toes.

Jesus. It was like a thousand icy pins pricking her feet.

Rain turned. "You've got to be kidding me."

"I'm sure it'll be fine."

He didn't look sure.

Rain took a deep breath and closed her eyes as she took a tepid step forward. Water covered her foot and splashed around her ankle. She locked her jaw to keep her teeth from chattering. *Think light. Think light.*

She took another step. This one lifted her out of the water and onto what felt like a patch of ice. Struggling to keep upright, Rain slid her feet over the surface, holding her arms out like a tightrope walker. She looked down.

Her feet, red from the cold, glided over the water. It was real. *She* was real. Something inside her burst open and flooded her body with warmth. Rain imagined that this was what *He* must have felt like two thousand years ago: terrified but filled with what could only be described as purpose. Worthwhile, all-consuming purpose.

When she looked up, smiling so wide it could have torn at the corners of her mouth, the four people on the other side of the pond stood still as statues, transfixed. Still not confident in her stride along the moving, slippery surface, Rain shuffled slowly across the pond toward them.

A fair-complexioned woman with round, brown eyes stepped forward from the group as Rain reached the opposite shore. "Wow."

"Tell me about it," Rain said.

Because he'd only partially fucked up his mistress's message, Belial was allowed to attend movie night. Occurring once every century or so, movie night was the single pleasure allowed the lower hordes, though, more often than not, the movies were of a sappy, gag-inducing sort. Still, to Belial, a movie was better than shit-mucking any day.

The movie hall was densely packed with others of his pay grade: Sputum Lake lifeguards, demons responsible for stubbed toes, and the three Sisters. No one knew what the sisters did exactly. Mostly, they wandered about Hell, leering and muttering.

Belial shoved his way toward the stage area—he was short and wouldn't be able to see squat otherwise—where General Drakul gazed over the crowd with his usual expression of disgust. Once the hall was full, he raised his hands. Obediently, the crowd quieted.

"I am here because it is the Mistress's wish that movie night be cancelled."

Growls erupted through the hall. Belial wouldn't dare express his anger within stabbing distance of the General, but it was impossible to hide the disappointment.

"Instead, you will be taking in live footage of the world above. This information is usually considered classified. Call it a treat." The General grinned.

"Treat, my asshole," a demon muttered behind Belial.

The Sisters stepped forward onto the stage. The oldest and ugliest plucked her right eye from the socket—no big deal. Belial's muck partner did the same as an antidote to boredom—and it began to glow colors he hadn't seen in centuries: blues and greens. A beam of light shot from the eye and lit up the wall where the movie would have been played. At first, the image was too fuzzy to make out, but as it cleared…

A small woman with hair like fire stood on the surface of a pond.

"Fuckin' 'ell," the demon behind Belial whispered.

"See? I told ya. That's her. Totally her," another said.

Belial turned to face them. "Her who?"

"You as stupid as you look?" the first said.

Belial reddened.

The second nudged the first. "What you want to bet they dunk her? Do that whole cleanse thing?"

"No doubt about it. Yes, sir, there'll be a dunk and then a war."

Then Belial understood. Even the lesser demons had a vague knowledge of the events meant to precede the Great War when the Mistress would take over the surface. This girl was what the goody-goods called the Messiah. The rules of engagement were clear: the Messiah must be without sin. A cleanse would sign her death warrant.

Belial watched with rapt attention, wondering if there would be proper movie nights when they finally went above.

CHAPTER THIRTEEN

ALERT THE MEDIA. CARVE IT in the record books. Stain it with blood. Lucy had been telling the truth. Judas didn't have time to analyze her step out of character. Rain stood on the opposite bank of the pond, chatting away as though nothing had changed. Only confirmed.

Son of a bitch.

No, son of God.

Same thing.

Anyone else would be elated. Dumbstruck. Much like the robe-clad twit bent over in the muck to slip sandals on Rain's feet. Judas, however, felt a gnawing combination of betrayal and panic.

"I get it," he muttered to the cloudy sky. "You work in mysterious ways and do not bend to the plan of a humble traitor. Lesson learned. You can let me in on what's going on now."

He waited. A goose, separated from its flock, landed nearby and picked at an abandoned pastry bag.

"You should take lessons from the Greeks." Judas pointed a finger at the goose. "You're shit at omens."

A stream of white dripped from the goose's backside.

"Fuck you, too."

Across the pond, one of the group members wrapped a faded white robe around Rain's shoulders and helped her to adjust the belt. At first, Judas thought they were only trying to warm her, but then the shortest of the group, a woman, led her by the elbow back to the water.

This can't be good.

Judas dropped her clothes on the damp grass and sprinted around the perimeter of the pond, reaching the group just as Rain waded knee deep.

"What the hell are you doing?" He forced the words through deep breaths. Two-thousand-year-old lungs were worse than a smoker's.

The woman guiding Rain shot him a nasty look.

"They're baptizing me," Rain said.

The one who'd put the sandals on her feet raised his Styrofoam cup. "It is written that John the Baptist baptized Jesus Christ. It is a sign that Rain should come to us on the very day that we are to baptize our sister in Christ, Maria."

Maria, a plain, young thing, waved meekly.

Judas turned to the woman holding Rain. "So you'd be John, then?"

"Stacy."

Judas covered his mouth and nose with his hands and pinched the bridge of his nose with his fingertips. He felt a headache brewing. "I really don't think this is a good idea," he said into his hands.

"What?" Rain said.

He removed his hands and clapped them together, once, loudly. "Out of the water, Rain."

Sandal-Boy stepped forward. "Who are you to order about the Messiah?"

"My agent," Rain said, apologetically. "Long story," she added when they all looked at her like she'd grown a second head.

The fourth of the group—a gray-haired, hook-nosed woman—silently watched from a distance. She didn't seem to care either way. Her face held no expression, and she stood as still as stone. The woman glanced at Judas, and it turned his stomach.

"Jude, it's cold. The longer we stand here arguing, the closer my legs are to falling off. I'm doing this. It's right."

Stacy and Sandal-Boy nodded triumphantly.

Short of dragging her out of the water, Judas couldn't stop her, and he was hesitant to manhandle the Messiah in front of her new followers. They'd probably drown him.

Waist-deep, Rain and Stacy turned to face the shore. Rain shivered, and her lips had already taken on a blue tinge.

Stacy held her in one arm and raised the other toward the sky. "Heavenly Father..."

Sandal-Boy and Maria bowed their heads. The hook-nosed woman and Judas stared forward.

"With this water, we humbly cleanse your messenger, our Messiah, of all sins. May she emerge a pure child of God. Amen."

"Amen," Sandal-Boy and Maria echoed.

Stacy dipped Rain backward into the frigid water and slipped, barely catching herself before she too was dunked. When she pulled Rain out, Judas noticed a bright red trickle from her arm.

Rain shivered violently. Stacy anxiously pulled her back to shore, where Sandal-Boy and Maria waited with a fresh robe, wearing twin looks of horror.

"Y-y-you cut the Messiah!" Sandal-Boy accused.

Stacy gasped.

Rain shook her head, teeth chattering. "It's f-fine. I h-hit a r-rock."

Judas snatched the robe from Maria and tucked Rain's thin form into it. He helped her slip out of her soaked jeans and wrapped another robe around her legs like a skirt. "I have a bad feeling about this," he whispered in her ear.

"What are you talking about?"

Judas looked over his shoulder at the hook-nosed woman. She hadn't moved since Rain entered the water, and her face was vacant. One of Lucy's scouts would have gone batshit by now, so she obviously wasn't one of them, but Judas knew the woman didn't belong there.

Stacy handed Judas a pair of sweatpants, head bowed to Rain. "Apologies, Messiah."

"Her name's Rain." Judas snatched the sweatpants.

"Thank you." Rain glared at Judas. Her shivering had slowed enough that she was able to dress herself.

The hook-nosed woman began to shudder.

Judas grabbed Rain's arm. "We have to go."

"Let us come with you," Stacy said.

Judas didn't give Rain the chance to respond. Still gripping her arm, he ran, practically dragging her behind him. After he'd put a few yards of distance between them and the woman, he chanced a look over his shoulder. The woman's clothes fell off in shreds. Skin bubbled and melted away. The explosive hum of thousands of wings hit Judas's ears, and he cried out in pain. Engorged, winged insects flew up out of the woman's insides and separated into swarms like black clouds. One of the clouds separated like a battalion and headed directly toward Judas and Rain.

Judas quickened his pace with Rain struggling to keep up. The robe flapped like a cape behind her. She looked behind them and screamed.

"What the hell are those things?"

"Locusts," Judas said.

Safely in the car, Judas threw it into reverse and stomped on the gas pedal. He needed to put as much distance between them and the swarm as possible. He needed time to think.

"What the fuck is a locust?" Rain stared gape-mouthed through the windshield.

"A problem."

They lost sight of the swarm once Jude lurched over a curb and hit the highway on-ramp at fifty miles per hour, but not before Rain watched a dozen of them fly down the throat of a man filling his gas tank. The man fell over the trunk of his car, eyes bulging out of his purple face.

"What's going on?" Rain asked.

Jude clutched the steering wheel, eyes darting between his mirrors.

Chills swept up and down her body. She reached forward and turned the heat on full blast. The sweatpants Stacy had given her were warm and dry but about two sizes too big. Rain yanked on the cords, pulling the elastic as tight as possible, and then tied them in a knot. She stripped out of the robe and reached into the backseat for her jacket. It was gone, and so were her shoes.

"My clothes?"

Jude looked startled. "I don't know. I must have dropped them." He turned and seemed to notice that she was soaked. "We'll get you something to wear."

"This isn't the way home. Where are we going?"

"My motel."

"Your motel?"

"It's safer there."

There was that panicked look again, the one she'd seen at the hospital. Jude's body was rigid, jaw clenched. Behind his eyes, Rain imagined she saw the wheels spin in manic rotations. This was not a man who was in control of the situation. This was a man who was just as lost as she was. Just as scared. The game had changed. Rain wondered if she could—should—trust him to lead her through it.

Her arm burned. She tried to peel the sleeve of her T-shirt up to examine the cut, but dried blood bonded the cotton to the wound. Through the wet material, Rain could tell the cut was long, but she didn't know how deep it went. There was blood everywhere, but she didn't feel dizzy and blamed her sickly pallor on the cold.

Rain bit her lip.

Like a Band-Aid. One. Two. *Riiiiiip.*

"Fuck," she gasped.

Jude grimaced. "That looks bad."

"It feels bad."

It started to bleed again. With no other options, Rain used the pond-water soaked robe belt as a bandage.

Jude pulled into the parking lot of a rundown Motel 6. Rain wondered how long he'd been staying there and why someone who could shell out so much cash was stuck sleeping in a roach motel. She moved to open the car door, but Jude stopped her.

"Have to be sure there aren't any of those flying fucks around," he said.

Rain nodded and suppressed the urge to gag. She would never be able to un-see what had happened to the man at the gas station.

Her stomach turned as she thought of how many more people had probably suffered the same fate.

"We should be okay. Just run," Jude said. "Go."

Rain flew from the car, slamming the door shut behind her. She followed Jude around the main office and down a sidewalk. He stopped at a room with brass numbers—three, zero—on the door and shakily slid his key into the lock. Once inside, Jude threw the door closed and blocked it with a chair.

Darkness shrouded the room, and it smelled like a thousand cigarettes had come there to die.

Jude flicked on the table lamp.

Pierced through its body with a sewing needle and pinned to the bedside table was a locust, deep brown and the size of Rain's hand. A note leaned against it with a blood red lip print.

"Jude..."

His eyes darkened. "I'll go to the office and see if they have a first-aid kit. You'll find clothes in that bag over there." He pointed to a duffel bag sitting on top of a chipped dresser then snatched up the locust and note. "Don't leave the room."

Rain said nothing.

Once Jude was gone and the sound of his footsteps barely above a whisper, Rain began rifling through every drawer, every crevice in the room in search of something to protect herself with. Someone had sent Jude a message. A female someone. And he hadn't looked shocked to see it. Just angry. Without a doubt, Jude was holding out on her.

In the bathroom garbage bin, she found a plastic fork. It was better than nothing. She slid it into the pocket of her sweatpants. Just in case.

CHAPTER FOURTEEN

JUDAS PELTED THE LOCUST AND Lucy's note into the row of bushes lining the parking lot. Her gloating didn't anger him as much as the fact that Rain had seen it. Now there would be questions, questions he wasn't prepared to answer. Part of him wanted to be honest: lay it all out for her to pick apart and deal with. But that was the idiot talking. He couldn't tell her anything without having a plan.

The way Judas saw it, he had two choices. He could let it all play out. Let the Messiah battle the Antichrist, whoever she was, and watch as the world collapsed around him. The problem with that, though, was that Lucy was right. Judas *did* know which side of the coin he would land on if that happened, and it wasn't the pretty one. On the other hand, he could make sure Rain didn't fight. No fight, no apocalypse. *Maybe* no apocalypse. He had no idea how it all worked. He hadn't *needed* to know until now.

His burning question, though, was why this was happening in the first place. Lucy claimed to have had one up on G, but Judas knew better. That wasn't possible. Was it? There was something else—someone else—in play. But who?

The desk clerk dug out an ancient-looking first-aid kit and handed it to Judas without a word. He rushed back to the room where Rain sat on the edge of the bed in sweatpants and one of the white T-shirts from his bag. She stared at the cut, tracing the perimeter of it with a dampened washcloth.

"I keep expecting it to heal instantaneously, like in the movies," she said without looking up at him.

Pity clawed at his chest. "Sorry. You're human. It has to heal the old-fashioned way."

Judas sat next to her and examined the cut. She'd done a decent job of cleaning it while he was in the office, but it was still nasty, jagged, and raw. In the first-aid kit, he found a small roll of gauze, bandages too thin to be of any use, tape, and a single alcohol wipe with the corner of the package ripped off. The wipe was half-dried, but it was better than nothing. Judas cleaned and dressed the cut with the gauze.

"You're good at that," Rain said.

"I've had a lot of practice."

The popular image of Joshua on earth was of a man without scars except for the ones left by Roman nails. In reality, the Son of God was a klutz, and Judas had always been the one to bandage his scrapes.

"I tried to heal myself." She blushed. "Didn't work, obviously."

"Of course it didn't."

Her eyes narrowed.

"He couldn't either."

"Oh."

A flicker of fear crossed Rain's face. Judas knew what she was thinking. If only Judas could reassure her that she wouldn't suffer the same fate. Reassure himself.

She crossed her arms. "So what was with the note? Girlfriend?"

He snorted. "Hardly."

She raised an eyebrow.

"It's complicated."

"Jude, there is a swarm of insects dive-bombing people's throats. You're going to need to give me a little more than that."

"It's really complicated." He sighed. "You're just going to have to trust me. I'll admit that I wasn't entirely expecting this, but that doesn't mean anything." *Yes it did,* he thought. God, the lies. "I'm working it out."

Rain didn't even try to pretend that she believed him. "You're full of shit."

He slammed his fist into the bed. "Damn it, Rain, just trust me, okay?"

"No. Not until you tell me what that message was about."

It was too soon for this. He closed his eyes. Counted to ten. He opened his eyes again and tried to smile reassuringly. "I understand. Really, I do. You're scared, and that's okay. But we're on the same team, here. I'm not going to turn on you."

Memories flashed of the night a bag, heavy with twenty pieces of silver, dropped into his hand.

Judas placed his hand on Rain's shoulder, which felt like a betrayal in and of itself. The lies were convincing even him.

After what felt like a long time, she nodded. "So what now?"

He gestured openhanded around the motel room.

Rain shook her head. "No. I'm not staying in here."

"Why not?"

"For one thing, there's an army of rodents in the walls and probably a body hidden in the mattress. Secondly, I can't just sit here. We have to warn people about the locusts."

"I'm sure they've figured it out by now."

"I'm serious. Maybe I can do something about it."

Doubt it. "Fine. But we're sticking to the indoors."

"Fine."

Judas pulled his second blazer from the bag for Rain. It fit, but over the T-shirt and sweatpants it looked ridiculous. She didn't seem to care.

He left the room first, looking and listening for any sign that the swarm had found its way to them. The sky was clear, and the only thing he heard was the garbled roar of a blasting television. Waving for her to follow, Judas jogged toward the parking lot.

Rain ran ahead, planting herself in front of the driver's side door. "Keys." She held out her hand.

"Excuse me?"

"If you want me to trust you, you're going to have to let me drive."

Judas had seen that look before. The *don't fuck with me* expression women wore was universal. It didn't comfort him. He tossed her the keys, and she quickly slid into the car. He rounded to the passenger side and pulled the handle.

Locked.

Rain started the car.

No.

"Open up!" Judas smacked his hand against the window. This couldn't be happening.

The car lurched forward, and Judas jumped out of the way, the rear tire barely missing his foot.

"Are you fucking serious?" he shouted after her.

The tires squealed as she took the corner onto the street and disappeared from view.

Judas stood there, gape-mouth flapping like a fish out of water, until another tenant walking toward his car said, "You okay?"

He nodded once.

The tenant flashed him a peace sign and climbed into his car.

Judas turned on his heel and walked mechanically back to the room. Without him, Rain was going to get herself killed. He started to wonder if he should care. Why did he even assume it was his responsibility to protect her? The whole plan had been turned inside out. Up was down, good was bad, and the figurehead was the real deal.

A throbbing pain began behind Judas's eyes and circled around his skull, where it hammered at the back of his head. He switched off the bedside lamp. It helped a little. With what little light shone through the cracks around the door, he found the painkillers tucked into the corner of the first-aid kit and swallowed four, dry.

A harried knock at the door pierced the dark.

Maybe she's not such an idiot after all.

Judas readied a tongue-lashing, opened the door, and then nearly choked on his unspoken words.

The pastor, Stacy, little-sister Mary, and Sandal-Boy stood in front of him, covered in mud.

Judas groaned. "What do you want?"

"We're here to see the Messiah." Sandal-Boy pulled a blade of grass from behind his ear. "We followed you two here after the... attack."

"She's not here." Judas pushed the door.

Stacy stuck her foot between the door and door jamb. "Then we'll wait. The Messiah showed herself to us. Being children of God, it is our duty to follow her until the End of Days."

Judas snorted. "Short trip, baby."

"Look, whoever you are, you can't keep us from her," Sandal-Boy said.

"Ashly!" Mary scolded.

So Sandal-Boy had a name, a girl's name at that. Fitting.

Mary maneuvered herself in front of the others. "Please. It's cold, and we're disgusting. Could we please come in?"

Judas sighed, stepping aside.

"Thank you." Mary crossed the threshold with a backpack over her shoulder.

The other two followed.

Ashly peeked into the bathroom. "She's not here."

"You assumed I was lying?"

He shrugged.

Mary disappeared into the bathroom with the backpack. The sound of the shower vibrated through the wall. Soon, steam drifted from beneath the door.

"Where did she go?" Stacy'd stripped out of her robe and managed to change her clothes without revealing an inch of skin. The woman was a contortionist.

"Your guess is as good as mine," Judas said.

"You lost her?" Ashly poked his head out from his own attempt at contortionism. It wasn't going as well. His legs were trapped in one side of his sweatpants, and his sweater had knotted itself around him like a straitjacket.

"No," Judas said.

"Then what happened to her?" Ashly demanded.

"She left."

Ashly's face fell. "She abandoned us?"

"*Me*. She abandoned *me*." *And good riddance to her.*

Stacy shoved Ashly's head back into the sweater while she tried to free him from it. "She wouldn't abandon us. She'll come back."

"You're expecting to wait here?" Judas rubbed his temples. The room was too small even for himself and Rain. One bed. One chair. Barely enough room to walk without tripping over things.

"Yes," Stacy said. "As were the Disciples of Christ, we are the Disciples of Rain."

"Ugh."

Freed, Ashly said, "Disciples of Rain. I like that. Catchy."

What a fucking nightmare. Maybe the end of the world wouldn't be such a bad thing after all. No, Judas couldn't let himself think like that. Hell would be infinitely worse than those three.

Mary emerged from the bathroom, dressed in clean jeans and a black hoodie, hair slicked back and tied up in an elaborate knot held in place by a pair of sticks. "What did I miss?"

"We're staying here," Ashly said.

"Fantastic. Is there food? I'm hungry."

Ashly whipped out a cell phone from his pocket. "Pizza?"

"No olives."

"And no peppers." Stacy held her hand out to Judas. "We should probably introduce ourselves properly."

"Jude." He took her hand.

Stacy pumped his hand once. "Lovely to meet you, Jude."

Mary pointed to the television. "Does this thing get cable?"

Judas didn't know whether to laugh or cry. They'd only an hour before witnessed a woman disintegrate into a swarm of locusts, and now their main concerns were olives on their pizza and the inadequacy of basic television. This was the humanity the Messiah was meant to save.

Of course, he'd known this already. He chose Rain on this very principle. She was part of a culture of jaded people but different enough that she could change it. The difference being that now it wasn't just their attitudes that hung in the balance.

CHAPTER FIFTEEN

I T WAS AS IF RAIN's foot on the accelerator had acted on its own. With Jude constantly hovering over her shoulder, she'd never be able to work out the truth of what was happening for herself, and it was at about a mile down the road that her mind caught up with her appendage, pleased with the action.

As she drove, she glanced continuously upward, looking and listening for the swarm. With no immediate threat, food became her number one priority. Rain had been living on coffee for the last twenty-four hours, and it felt as though the lining of her stomach was corroding. She needed something, anything, to staunch the burn.

The pastel sign of a small bakery rose over a patch of trees to her right. She pulled into the parking lot, surprised to see business as usual. Maybe the swarm had dissipated, or perhaps it wasn't as large as she'd thought. Or it just hadn't reached this far yet.

Angel Food Bakery, it was called.

A sprinkling of patrons littered the booths inside, leaving only the coffee bar as a place to sit. Rain would have preferred to be in the corner, away from prying eyes. The staring was blatant. Not that she blamed them. She looked like a hobo and probably stank. She folded her arms over her chest, trying to be as small as possible. Now was one of those times she regretted her choice of hair color.

Rain sat on a chrome stool upholstered in white vinyl. Just behind the bar was a workstation where platters of cupcakes cooled, waiting to be iced and decorated. Off to the side, a dark-haired woman in a white chef's coat chiseled at layers of marble cake. Cookies, wide and stacked high, taunted Rain from behind Plexiglas.

Her mouth watered.

A familiar blonde woman emerged from behind a door in the back. She looked up from the ledger in her hands, and upon locking eyes with Rain, she stopped mid-step. Her face faltered before her lips turned up at the corners into a forced smile.

Rain couldn't tell whether the woman was angry or startled at her presence.

She placed the ledger beneath the counter and draped an apron around her neck. "How can I help you?"

Rain studied the woman's features. Where had she seen the woman before? "I can't decide. Everything looks amazing," she said, hoping to brighten the woman's demeanor.

The fake smile didn't budge. "Will it just be, uh, are you alone, or will someone be joining you?" The woman looked anxiously toward the door.

Rain followed her gaze. "No. It's just me."

"Oh. All right." Her eyes brightened. Her skin brightened. The woman seemed to glow despite the soft lighting.

Then Rain recognized her. The woman from the park. The one who'd stepped in the way of a demon.

"You're... you're a..."

The woman shushed her. "My name is Lily. Just Lily."

She turned, and Rain gazed at her face in profile. The sharp swoop of a nose. Dimple. Recognition lit her up inside. She'd seen Lily as a child. Watching. Interfering when her mother got out of control.

"Lily, were you—"

She shot Rain a warning look. "Not important. You're hungry."

Rain's stomach growled loud enough for everyone to hear.

Wielding a flat blade, Lily chose the largest of the batch of cupcakes in front of her and expertly spread white icing over the top. Over that, she sprinkled flakes of red sugar and dark chocolate shavings. As a garnish, she topped it with a white chocolate cross.

It looked both delicious and morbid.

Lily placed the finished treat on a white china plate and slid it across the bar to Rain.

"Are you trying to tell me something?"

Lily frowned. "And what would I have to tell a stranger that could be said via cupcake?" She wrapped a plastic fork in a napkin and set it next to the plate. "Something to drink?"

"Water, please."

She nodded and left to retrieve it.

Rain unfolded the napkin. Inside, scrawled almost illegibly was: *Stay away from her.*

Her?

Rain slipped the napkin into her pocket and, foregoing the fork, took a mouth-filling bite of the cupcake. Rain moaned with pleasure. It was heavenly.

Several minutes passed before Lily returned with a glass. Rain had finished eating. Sated, she was ready to start asking questions.

Lily placed the glass in front of Rain, wearing a grim expression.

In the glass was a red liquid, too dark and too thick to be wine.

"It's started," Lily whispered.

"What's started? What is this?"

"It came from the tap. The water. It isn't water anymore. It's blood."

Nausea hammered Rain's stomach. She launched herself from the stool, knocking it over, and ran past the booths toward what she hoped was a bathroom. She'd only just opened the door when she started to heave. Masticated cupcake bits rode a river of green bile into the toilet. Blood had never had this effect on her before, but seeing it served up in a glass, imagining the feel of it trickling down her throat, the copper taste—it was too much.

Rain wiped her mouth on some toilet paper and flushed. The bowl refilled with blood. Panicked, she turned on the faucet. Blood spilled from the spigot.

When she emerged from the bathroom, the bakery was empty. No patrons. No Lily. Not even a cookie crumb. Dank and dusty, it looked as though there hadn't been a soul inside the building in years.

Out the window, Jude's car was just as she left it, but the sign for

Angel Food Bakery was gone. In the sky, parallel to the sun, was a full moon shining as brightly as it would in the middle of the night.

The three self-named Disciples of Rain sat cross-legged on the bed with slices of pizza paused in mid-air en route to their mouths, eyes glued to the television where a rerun of *Family Matters* had been interrupted by a Special News Bulletin. Judas paced beside the bed, chewing the side of his thumb.

Mary offered him a thin slice of pepperoni. He declined, stomach in knots.

The reporter stood in front of a Walmart Supercenter where hundreds of people piled into the store, emerging with gallons of water.

He yelled into the microphone to be heard over the noise. "It was only moments ago that Minneapolis exterminators were able to contain the unusual single-swarm migration of African locusts to a manageable level. Now, officials are baffled by the latest turn of events. The city water treatment plants in the Twin Cities unexpectedly shut down, only to restart seconds later; but instead of churning out clean, drinkable water, citizens turned on their faucets and showers to discover a red liquid resembling blood coming into their homes and businesses."

Ashly dropped his pizza in his lap. "Jesus Christ."

"Shut up." Judas rushed to the television to turn up the volume.

Mary went to the bathroom. Judas heard water rushing into the sink. He held his breath.

"Water." She rejoined the group on the bed.

The reporter continued, "Specialists have been called in to test the liquid but are not optimistic as to what they will find. Officials urge citizens to stock up on bottled water and to keep their faucets turned off."

Behind the reporter, Judas noticed a man with a large pack strapped to his back, the kind with buckles that wrapped around his torso. He wore army fatigues and a black beret on his bald head. It wasn't his appearance that gave Judas pause. The man was too calm. While everyone around him rushed past with carts, dragging bewildered children behind them, he stood still, barely in the frame.

The door handle jiggled, followed by three hard, rapid knocks.

"More of your friends?" Judas asked Stacy.

She shook her head.

Judas had no weapon. The best he could come up with was a rusted coffee pot that looked as though it hadn't been used in years. He raised it over his head, clutched the door handle, turned it, and prepared to swing.

Rain. Her face was ghostly white. She waved weakly.

He didn't lower the pot.

"Are you going to let me in?"

Judas didn't have time to consider his answer. At the sound of her voice, the Disciples leapt from the bed and crowded the door.

"Where have you been?" Ashly reached out to touch her limp arm.

"We were worried." Stacy pushed Ashly to the back of the group.

"You look rough," Mary said.

Stacy pried the pot from Judas's hand and pulled Rain inside toward the bed. "Here. Rest."

Rain sat at the edge of the bed with her hands folded in her lap. There was something crusted at the corner of her mouth. Judas stood next to the bed and watched her while the Disciples rounded the bed and resumed their positions.

A commercial for laundry detergent ended, and the reporter in front of the Walmart smiled forcibly into the camera. The man with the beret hadn't moved.

Rain's eyes widened, and she sat up a little straighter.

"What is it?" Judas murmured into her ear. He was pretty sure the three stooges were harmless, but he didn't exactly trust them. If there was any hope of getting them off Rain's back, alerting them to trouble would destroy it.

"Sycamore," she said.

"What?"

She stood. "We have to get down there."

"Why?"

"My brother... he's going to—oh no."

Judas turned to the television. The man had turned to face the camera and stared daggers into it. Above his head, he held a handwritten sign, red letters on white poster board. *I speak for Messiah. You have polluted your water. Now drown in it.*

"Hippie garbage," Ashly spat.

"He couldn't possibly mean Rain," Stacy said.

"Brother?" Judas sat next to Rain. More fucking secrets. It's as though they came from every angle just to piss him off. "What aren't you telling me?"

The reporter stood to the side, and the camera zoomed in on the man's sign. Upon closer inspection, it looked as if it'd been written in blood.

"It's my mother," she said, unblinking eyes still staring at the television.

"I thought you said it was your brother."

"No. Messiah. The one that detective mistook me for? It's her. It's my mother. She's been going around with an orange wig cut like my hair."

"Why would she do that?"

Rain shook her head. "Something bad is going to happen. We need to call the cops or something. Call that detective. Get those people out of there."

"He's just protesting," Mary interjected.

"No." Rain turned to look at her. "He's not."

As though on cue, a bone-rattling bang erupted from the television. Judas looked just in time to see bits of the man Rain called Sycamore fly over the crowd before the camera went black.

Nobody spoke. The only sound was Ashly's rapid breathing.

Judas's mind was like an unfinished puzzle. He had a general idea of what the picture was going to be, but there were pieces missing that skewed his perception. Rain's admission that her mom was the false Messiah was a crucial piece. It slid into place, revealing a portion of the picture.

Lucy had made a point to correct him when he had assumed the Antichrist was male. Seemed smug about it, too.

It was her. Had to be. Rain's mother was the Antichrist.

Knowing this, though, only left Judas with more questions, more mismatched puzzle pieces. Why the whole charade of a figurehead Messiah? Why Judas? And why did he get the feeling there was someone else pulling existential strings around him? God, he was tired of getting dicked around.

Rain made a beeline for the room's telephone. She lifted the receiver only to have Judas slam his finger down on the hook.

"What are you doing?"

"I'm calling that detective. Someone has to put a stop to this."

"That's not going to help."

"Oh? And why not?"

Judas looked up into the faces of the Disciples, hanging on his and Rain's every word. "Excuse us," he said with a curt nod.

He gripped Rain by the arm.

Ashly stood. Judas shot him a look. "Down, boy." He slipped a key card into his back pocket before escorting Rain out of the room.

Outside, Judas relinquished his grip on her arm, but stood close enough to smell the old vomit on her breath. He wouldn't underestimate her this time. He knew she would try to slip away the first moment she could.

"What is your problem?"

"Rain, this isn't something that detective can fix."

"It is! When they took me, they brought me to the house I grew up in. I could tell the detective where to find it, she can bring backup, and this will all be over."

Of course. The demons he'd sensed in the van were working for her mother. And G had let it happen. Christ, she could have been killed. Or worse.

"No. It's bigger than that,"

"How?"

"The locusts, the blood... this is only the beginning. Rain, it's happening. The Antichrist is here."

"But you said—"

"I know what I said. I was working under false assumptions."

A snarl curled her lip. "You don't have a clue what's going on."

"I know that the apocalypse has begun."

Saying it out loud stole the air from his lungs. He felt in over his head.

Rain turned and stormed down the covered walkway. Judas had to jog to keep up with her.

"Listen," he said, already out of breath. Fucking body. "You need to lay low for a while, at least until we understand this better."

"That's not an option."

"You're not ready for this."

"Yeah, well, you should have thought of that when you put that ad in the paper. Do you have any idea how many people showed up at my apartment looking for my help? I panicked!"

Ad?

"What are you talking about?"

She slowed but didn't stop. "The ad in the paper that provided the entire fucking world with my home address."

"I didn't put an ad in the paper. Why would I do that?"

"If you didn't, then who did?"

Rain turned her head to face the parking lot and gasped. Judas turned to see what she was looking at. His face burned with white-hot anger as another jagged puzzle piece fell into place.

Francine sat on the hood of the car, leaning back against the windshield with her legs crossed at the ankle. Her tank top and jeans left nothing to the imagination, and her hair was piled atop her head, curls shooting out of the hairband like red fireworks.

She raised her hand and giggled. "Guilty."

CHAPTER SIXTEEN

JUDAS COULDN'T HELP NOTICING THE way Francine's ankle twitched. She didn't seem to care. She was too busy basking in the flames of his anger.

Rain was rigid. Her arms locked as though she worried what would happen if she didn't keep them at her side. Judas wouldn't blame her if she throttled Francine. He certainly wanted to.

"I don't understand," Rain said.

"Understand what, sweetie?" Francine slid off the hood of the car, slinked toward Rain, and tried to embrace her.

Rain took a step back.

"Why would you do that? It... it doesn't make any sense."

"Sure it does." Judas positioned himself between the two women, his back to Rain. "She wanted to make sure your mother found you."

"What does my mother have to do with anything?"

Francine smiled. "Everything."

Judas took Rain's hand and pulled her in the direction of the room. "We'll talk inside."

Her eyes never left Francine. Judas could tell in the way Rain's face flushed and how many times she blinked back tears that she was fighting herself. The poor girl had gone and fallen in love with the bitch. As they walked with Francine following behind, Rain stole glances over her shoulder. He felt Francine's eyes pierce the back of his skull.

Back in the room, Mary and Stacy eyed Francine with immediate suspicion. Ashly's tongue had to be rolled back in his mouth. Rain stood near the door, arms crossed, while Francine played with her hair. Judas resisted the urge to break her hands. That she'd somehow manipulated Rain into falling for her was disgusting, but the way he'd allowed her to play him for a fool pushed Judas to the border of homicide.

Stacy stood next to Judas, sneering. "Who's she?"

The woman was starting to grow on him. "Her name's Francine. She's a fallen angel."

The blood fell from Rain's face, and she tottered. Mary jumped from the bed and held Rain up by the waist while she rested her head on Mary's shoulder.

"A demon?" Ashly's face fell.

"No," Francine began.

"Close enough," Judas said.

Francine sniffed, pushing her chin up in the air. "A Grigori."

Mary and Ashly looked to Stacy, who turned to Rain. The Messiah pried herself out of Mary's hold and walked shakily toward the other side of the room. "Need to sit down." She sank into the chair with her head between her legs.

Judas wondered if Rain would be able to handle full knowledge. She'd looked bad when she came back from running off with the car. Something had happened to Rain while she'd been gone. He'd never get it out of her while Francine was around.

Stacy nodded. "Yes, the Grigori. Banished to the Earth for pursuing sins of the flesh rather than keep vigilance over mankind."

"That's them." Judas kept Rain in the corner of his eye where he could watch her.

Francine turned in a circle, presumably so the Disciples could get a good look.

Judas threw a cup at Ashly. "Don't get any ideas, Sunshine. That cunt is evil."

"You would know." Francine licked her lips.

He cringed.

Rain groaned.

"That was centuries ago," Judas reminded Francine but more for Rain's benefit. He needed her on his side.

Rain sat up in the chair. Her breathing was off, and she seemed to be having a hard time looking at Francine. "Why did you…" She shook her head. "What does my mother have to do with you?"

"Rain, I think that you and I—"

"Oh shut up, Judas. She asked me."

There was a collective intake of breath.

Francine laughed. "Wait. Don't tell me they don't know who you are."

The Disciples gathered in a half circle around Rain with her at the front. He didn't give a shit what they thought of him, but Rain's glare was damning.

"I can explain," he said before any sort of explanation could be formed.

Francine joined the half circle around Rain next to Ashly. "You can explain how the greatest traitor of all time came to be in the company of the Messiah?" She winked then turned to Rain. "Let me paint you a picture of white walls and a room with no door. A white hell for the traitor. A hell he would do anything to get out of, including sacrifice a random girl—"

Judas snarled. "You traitorous bitch. You know whose idea it was to—"

"Now, now, Judas. You're deflecting. Just accept that you've been found out and slink back to your little cave."

"Please," he said to Rain. "Just listen. It's not what you think."

"Get out," Rain said through clenched teeth.

"It's my motel room." Even to his own ears, it sounded childish.

Francine stroked Rain's shoulder, eyes on Judas. "I think you should leave."

He tried to move around her, but the others closed in tighter around their leader. Not that it mattered. Rain wasn't even looking at him now.

"Fine. I'll go." Judas locked onto Francine's eyes and found it impossible to convey exactly how much she repulsed him. "This isn't over."

She smiled. "Sadly, it is."

Looking to Stacy with a final wordless plea, he was met with icy stares. If they wouldn't listen to him, he needed a new plan.

With watchful glares on him from every direction, he snaked his hand into the pocket of the blazer Rain still wore and pulled out the car keys.

"Be careful," he whispered.

The quiet was too loud. Rain wished everyone would just shut up. Jude—Judas, she corrected herself—was gone, and at the time, kicking him out seemed like a good decision. It still did, but it did nothing to relieve the tension behind her eyes.

With a look, Francine sent the Disciples outside. Mary and Stacy wore sympathetic grins while Ashly's tongue still lolled in lust for this woman who apparently wasn't a woman after all.

Glancing up at Francine while Rain's gaze was fixed on the departing Disciples, Rain accepted that this wasn't *her* Francine, and in that acceptance she reached a profound sadness. *Her* Francine had never really existed. It was a feeling so dark and cold and buried beneath it all that it didn't even have a word. It just was, and it was suffocating.

"Finally we can have a moment alone." Francine sighed and lowered herself onto the bed, stretching her limbs like a cat preparing for an afternoon nap.

"Ugh."

"Don't be mad at me, lover. I had to go away for a while."

Rain flinched at the word *lover* as though she'd been smacked. "I think you should leave, too."

Her eyes widened. "Leave?"

Rain fixed her gaze on a cigarette burn in the carpet. If she looked at Francine, what little resolve she'd summoned would dissolve. She nodded.

"You don't mean that."

"I do."

"I'm still me." Francine slid from the bed to the floor and into

Rain's direct line of vision. She pried Rain's hand from the arm of the chair and held it against her cheek.

Cold, like a pillow left by an open window.

"What about my mother?" The image of her brother's body exploding stained on the back of her mind. This was her only chance for answers. The problem, of course, was that she didn't know if she would be able to trust the answers. Rain pulled her hand from Francine's grasp.

Francine's smile didn't waver. "What about her?"

"You said it has everything to do with her. Why?"

"What did Judas tell you about the apocalypse?"

"Why can't you just answer my question?"

"Why can't you answer me?"

Rain sat up straighter. "Tell me."

Francine's eyes darkened. "Fine. I'd wager he told you that it wouldn't begin without the Antichrist's presence, yes? That it wouldn't happen because of... special circumstances?"

Rain didn't need to answer. She was sure Francine could read the confirmation on her face. Like it or not, Francine knew Rain.

"He was right. It takes both light and dark to ignite the cosmic fuse. But he lied to you when he said it wouldn't happen. It is happening, obviously. So that can only mean that he lied to you about the presence of the Antichrist."

At that moment, Rain was thankful for the chair.

Francine continued, "It's your mother."

A sob and a laugh escaped Rain's mouth at the same time, coming out as a sort of hiccup. Every child at one point in their life swears that a parent is the devil sent to Earth to torture them. How lucky that she would be the one who was right! No, lucky implied coincidence, a concept Rain was slowly starting to believe was complete bullshit.

"Judas said you wanted to ensure she found me."

Francine stood and looked down at her. "He's a liar."

"So are you."

She stiffened. "I had to lie. To protect you."

"Protect me? From what?"

An instant's hesitation. A confident smirk. "Not a lot of people are familiar with the name Grigori. Most people call us Watchers. Apt name because that's what we did. We watched. It was our duty to watch over humanity. To protect them from Hell's hordes."

An image flashed in Rain's mind of the woman in the park. Lily.

"We spent so much time around your kind that it was only natural some of us fell in love." She paused. Sighed. "We were punished for it. Banished to Earth. We became human. Well, some of us. I know, to you, that doesn't sound like punishment, but for us—them—it was worse than death. I was granted mercy... of a sort. Until the End of Days, I cannot return home, but I was allowed my proper form. And it is in this form that I am able to protect you from the hordes. I needed to protect you because I fell in love with you."

Her words rang with sincerity, and her smile was natural. They said that eyes were windows into the soul. Francine's were shrouded. Rain wanted so badly to believe her.

"Rain!" One of the Disciples called through the door.

"Leave them," Francine ordered. "Please," she added, softer.

Be careful, he'd said to her.

"Can I trust you?" Rain knew it was a pointless question, but still. Emotion made idiots of everyone.

"Of course."

"It's cold outside. We'll let them in. You can stay."

Francine smiled triumphantly. It should have warmed Rain's heart. Instead, it frightened her.

CHAPTER SEVENTEEN

MARY AND ASHLY LOOKED AT Judas with less repugnance now that they'd been banished from the room as well.

Stacy studied him, lips pursed. "You don't look how I imagined."

"Don't believe everything you see on television. None of us looked like Al Pacino," Judas said, ear to the door.

"No, that's the devil," Ashly said.

"She doesn't look like him either."

"Knew it."

"Shut up, Ashly," Mary said.

"All of you shut up." Judas stuck a finger in his other ear. There wasn't time for this.

Fucking manipulative bitch. He could only hear half of what she was saying, but he knew Rain was falling for all of it. None of it mattered to him, though, except one seemingly innocuous admission: *until the End of Days, I cannot return home...*

So that was Francine's game. End the world so that she could suckle at the glowing *hallelujah* tit again. She had to know what would happen to Rain if that was allowed to happen.

Judas swore through clenched teeth.

"What is it?" Stacy's face was screwed up in thought. Maybe he would use her.

"Francine is going to try to manipulate Rain into accelerating the events of the apocalypse. If that happens, Rain will die."

Mary gasped. Ashly looked at his feet.

Stacy's gaze didn't waver. "But that is how it is written. The End of Days is inevitable."

"Yes, but it isn't supposed to happen now. The wheels were put into motion too soon."

"How do you know?"

He shook his head. "You'll just have to trust me."

"Sayeth Judas."

"Oh, for fuck's sake, Stacy, just listen to me. Rain is a good person and doesn't deserve this. Francine is an angel, yes, but one who has fallen from grace. Can you even imagine what it would do to a being like that? To be *created* to serve and then cast off like yesterday's garbage? It's changed her. She's two horns and a forked tail away from her own place in Lucifer's army."

Stacy shook her head.

Mary seemed to have no problem believing this, though, nodding along with Judas's tirade. "What do you want us to do?"

"Don't let Francine into Rain's head. Most importantly, don't let Rain fight."

"And what are you going to do?"

"Try to stop this."

"How?"

Judas shrugged. "No idea."

The door opened and Rain gestured for the Disciples to enter. Francine's arm ensnared her neck like a noose.

Judas sat in the car for a long time, eyeing the motel through the rearview mirror, itching to storm back into the room to see if angels bled red. How could he have been so stupid as to trust her? Who was Judas kidding? If Lucy herself had walked into that godforsaken white room and offered a chance to leave, he would have taken it.

He turned the key, and the car shuddered to life. The idling hum helped focus his thoughts into two categories: what he knew and what he needed to know.

Judas knew that the process had begun. The Antichrist and the

Messiah were both on Earth and now, thanks to Francine, aware of each other. He knew that the plagues had begun.

He didn't know how to stop them or what would follow.

He knew that Plague, the Horseman, was the only entity capable of bringing them. He knew that he needed to find Plague and somehow stop him from setting his final contributions upon the Earth and thereby paving the way for his three cohorts.

Judas rubbed his eyes, taking deep, controlled breaths. All he had to do was stop Plague with no weapons, no power, and no idea where to find him.

Sure. No problem.

The best place to start, Judas figured, was the water treatment plant where the blood had first appeared. Locust woman had been a pawn, a tool for the first Horseman. Nothing would be gained from going back to the lake. He knew better than to hope that Plague would still be hanging around, but maybe he'd be able to follow his footsteps. Everything left a mark.

Judas stopped at a gas station, recently abandoned by the look of it, and made a phone call to directory assistance. Number and address in hand, he snatched a map of the city from a display, leaving a dollar on the counter.

The outer gates of the treatment plant were blocked by a pair of police cars with flashing lights when Judas arrived. He hadn't thought about getting past the cavalry. He parked in a lot across the street and checked his appearance in the side mirror. The suit was miraculously clean and wrinkle-free. If he managed to keep his head low, Judas could pass for a person who was supposed to be there. An inspector, maybe. It'd be better if he carried a briefcase or clipboard. In the trunk, he found an empty manila folder that was bent at the corners.

Good enough.

Judas approached the gate. Two police officers were too occupied with a trio of people in silver hazmat suits to notice him as he slid past. The security post at the center of the gate was empty, but it probably wouldn't be for much longer. Judas sneaked in, snatched a stack of official looking paperwork, and hung a visitor badge around his neck.

The police finished their business with the hazmat guys who were fast approaching Judas. Donning an appropriate scowl of annoyance at having been dragged from his office to deal with the situation, he fell in step behind them.

"I'm telling you, man, this is it," the line leader said.

"Don't be stupid, Ernie. It's just some psycho green freaks trying to make a point. Bet you anything it's food dye."

"Gallons of food dye being rolled inside in broad daylight, you'd think someone would've noticed."

"Still..." The third crossed himself with his gloved hand. "Make your peace now."

"I'll give you a piece," the second said, chuckling.

At Ernie's count of three, the men opened the doors leading into the lobby. It was void of life and rightfully so. The stench of dead, rotting meat knocked the wind out of him. Judas bent over and gagged.

The hazmat guys turned to face him.

"Who the hell are you?"

"Inspe—" He gagged again, unable to get the word out.

"Someone give him a mask or something, jeez."

A thin, white medical mask was extracted from one of their packs and passed to Judas. It didn't completely block the smell, but at least he could breathe.

"Thank you," he said. "I'm an inspector for the city."

The first laughed. "Well, Mr. Inspector, I think you're a little late."

Judas glared. "I'll take your name and supervisor then."

The third put his hands up. "Okay, okay. Be my guest. I'm not exactly looking forward to going in there."

"Still think it's food dye?" Ernie said.

"Shut up."

"All of you," Judas said, "shut up. Where did they say the initial dump was?"

"Shouldn't you know that, Mr. Inspector?"

Ernie elbowed Smartass. "Pool A. Through there." He pointed to a set of double doors. "Just follow the hallway."

Judas nodded and walked in the direction Ernie'd pointed with the others snickering behind him. In an earlier life, he would have shown Smartass exactly why he should make peace with whatever god he looked to in a crisis. But considering the task at hand, it would have been counterproductive. Besides, if Plague couldn't be dealt with, Smartass would see for himself soon enough.

The hall to Pool A was only partially lit by flickering lights. Judas listened for the hum of an air conditioner. Nothing. They'd probably cut the main power in an attempt to stall the contamination. It would only work for so long. The Horsemen were resourceful. They'd been training for this their entire existence. It was the *one thing* they were meant to do.

And then Judas had an idea. It'd be impossible to defeat them by physical means, but he could talk to them. If there was anything Judas knew how to do, it was talk.

The door was secured by a digital lock, but someone had broken the keypad. He heard buzzing through the crack.

Plague should have moved on by now. What was he waiting for?

Judas slipped the mask over his head then waited for the nausea to pass before prying the door open.

Plague sat at the edge of the platform in a more or less human shape, dangling leg-like appendages over the side. Streams of red fell from them, darkening the already bloodied pool. His clothes—a mud-stained T-shirt and jeans—trembled as various creepy-crawlies crept beneath the material. His head morphed between round and oval as the locusts that made him up wandered over each other.

"I know you," he said, voice like the hum of a swarm.

"I'm flattered."

Plague laughed, and it looked as though his head exploded with the effort. The locusts settled back onto his swaying neck. "Don't be."

"Fair enough." Judas dropped the paperwork and mask next to the door and approached Plague. "May I sit?"

The locusts forming Plague's shoulders lifted in uneven points meant to resemble a shrug.

Judas suppressed a shudder. He sat back from the edge, keeping his long legs inches from the surface of the pool. "I'm surprised to see you here."

"The End of Days has begun."

"No, of course I know that. I mean I'm surprised to see you still here. I'd think you'd be pelting frogs into the streets by now."

Plague didn't respond.

Judas probed further. "The humans have already dealt with the swarm, and it won't be much longer before all this is flushed..."

"Be gone."

"I'm not criticizing, Plague. It's good work."

"Damn right it is."

"So then what's the hold up, if you don't mind my asking?"

Another pseudo-shrug.

"If you want my opinion—"

"I don't." Plague kicked at the surface, sending a spray of blood that splattered like a murder scene across the outer walls.

Judas took a deep breath. He was pushing it. "My opinion is that you ought to get this nonsense over with so you can move on to bigger and better things."

"There's nothing after this. Nothing!"

"That's a good point."

Plague looked up at Judas. He had no face, only a slit where his voice carried the echoes of locust wings. "Insects. Blood. Frogs. These are what I have to deface a planet that's done more damage to itself than I could cause in a thousand years."

"Don't sell yourself short."

"Shut it, traitor. Once I finish this, there's nothing left for me. I'll have no purpose."

"I see what you mean."

"You see nothing," Plague snapped.

A pair of locusts flew from his face and onto Judas's hand. It took everything he had not to shake them off. "Might I offer a suggestion?"

"As if I have a choice."

"Don't finish."

Plague paused. The locusts on his face lifted their wings, buzzing excitedly.

"You've seen the humans in action and what they can handle. Given enough time and creativity, you can show them what Plague is made of. They will cower beneath the waves of destruction you create."

"I'm under orders."

"Whose orders?"

"I will not speak her name."

Judas was almost there. "This approach into the End of Days is tainted. You know this. It's why you're still sitting here, moping. Give it time. Don't let yourself be a joke."

Plague stood. Judas remained seated, allowing Plague to view himself as above him.

"You're right, traitor."

"What are you going to do?"

The corners of the slit in his mouth turned upward. "Like the sleeping dragon, I shall lie in wait until the time of Man is to be over."

Judas nodded. "Ah, great. Fantastic. See you then."

Plague's clothes ripped away as the locusts fell out of his man-like form and tumbled over Judas. He took flight as a swarm, sweeping gracefully out of the pool room.

The warm, raw meat stink from the pool grew more noticeable now that Judas wasn't distracted. He stood, collected the paperwork to ensure a smooth exit, and replaced the mask over his face.

One down, three to go.

CHAPTER EIGHTEEN

FRANCINE WOULDN'T ALLOW RAIN TO let the Disciples in on her own. Before all of this, Rain would have begged to have her hands never leave her body. Now, Francine's arms were like snakes, her fingers like the probing touch of spider legs. Rain didn't fight it, though. The words she'd waited so long to hear had finally been uttered. Maybe now Francine was finally being honest. Maybe this time it would be different.

Ashly and Stacy stayed by the door, eyeing the angel warily.

Mary stood next to Rain and took her hand. "You don't look so hot."

Francine sliced her body between them. "She's fine. Just tired."

Rain took a step back. "I watched my brother blow himself up on the local news. I'm angry. I'm sad. I'm anything but tired."

This was only a partial lie. She was all those things *and* worn out. Rest wasn't an option though. "I need to go back to my mother's house."

"Did you miss the part about your mother being the Antichrist?" Mary asked.

"My sister is there. Something could happen. A bomb..." She blinked back tears.

Rain knew River would only do such a thing if she were forced. But with her mother's eager foot soldier gone, it was just a matter of time before her sister's insides were displayed for the benefit of the local news.

Francine kissed her shoulder. "That's not a good idea, my love. There are... steps... one must take during such a delicate situation."

"Like?" Rain snapped.

"You aren't to meet the Antichrist until the End, where you will fight for the souls of the human race. And mine."

"Heavy," Ashly muttered.

"I'm not fighting," Rain said.

"You don't understand. You have to," Francine insisted.

Rain brushed her off. "I don't care."

Francine's face darkened. "Rain—"

"You said you love me, so help me. If you care at all,"—*or are pretending to care*—"you'll help me do this."

"I'm in." Mary glared at Stacy and Ashly until they mumbled their agreement.

Outvoted, Francine nodded once, scowling. "When?"

"Now." Rain dug through Judas's duffel for different clothes.

Mary handed her a hoodie from one of the Disciple's bags.

"Fine." Francine headed for the bathroom.

"What are you doing?"

"Fallen angels do occasionally need to piss."

"Oh."

When Francine emerged several minutes later, tucking a phone into her back pocket, the scowl had been become a smirk, and there were no more objections.

Night sneaked in like a thief, stealing what was left of solid daylight while Judas drove deeper into the heart of the city, considering his next move.

He was alone on the road. The blood contamination had reached far enough that most people sought shelter in their homes, hoarding their stock of bottled spring water. Every storefront and restaurant he passed was closed, a fact Judas swallowed with frustration as his stomach growled. He should have snatched a muffin or something when he had the chance.

Plague seemed to have moved on to whatever plain of existence he came from. Judas hadn't seen a swarm straggler since the morning, and the air felt lighter. He didn't harbor any delusions that it would last though. Plague was a pawn on Lucy's board. Judas could almost hear her laughing at him.

Around the next corner, Judas spotted a man lounging on a stool behind a hotdog cart. He was either an optimist or an idiot. But whatever the case, he had food, and for that, Judas was thankful.

He pulled the car along the curb—no one was going to care about illegal parking today—and approached the man. He was like a beach ball with appendages whistling the melody to "Twinkle, Twinkle, Little Star."

When the man saw Judas, he smiled widely and saluted. Judas didn't know whether he ought to salute back or ignore the gesture. He nodded.

"A sight for sore eyes, good sir," the man said.

"The feeling is mutual."

"What'll it be then? Footlong? Sausage?"

"Both," Judas said, glad he had long since renounced his people's aversion to pork.

The man continued to whistle.

"Not that I'm not grateful, but can I ask what you're even doing out here?"

"End of the world or not, a man's gotta feed his family."

Judas nodded and slid an extra twenty dollars into the man's hand. "Watch yourself."

"Always do."

Food in hand, Judas headed back to the car. He gazed upward at a full, crimson moon and bit into the hotdog. The skin made a satisfying snap in his mouth, and ketchup gushed into the corners of his mouth.

The second bite turned to ash in his mouth. He gagged and scraped his tongue with his fingernails. Famine, the second Horseman, hadn't wasted any time.

"Couldn't let me have just one fucking hotdog, could you?" he yelled into the night.

A high-pitched giggle rode the wind, swirled around him, and headed east.

Behind him, the cart vendor had disappeared. Judas felt a stab of regret.

Knowing what would become of the sausage he still held, no matter how delectable it smelled, he tossed it into a nearby trash bin. His stomach growled again.

Judas climbed in the driver's side. Lucy greeted him from the passenger seat with a vicious grin. He jumped and then scolded himself for letting her sneak up on him like that. Judas had figured she would come to him eventually, but he'd hoped that at least two of the Horseman would be taken care of by then.

"I hear you're being a bad boy." Her breath smelled like scorched dirt.

"*Bad* implies that there are rules to follow. You and I both know those have gone out the fucking window."

Lucy slid her hand over the center console and onto his leg. Her fingers morphed into thin, black snakes that probed his inner thigh, working their way upward to his—

"Ach!"

She giggled. "Looks like they found a friend."

"No matter what you may have heard about my people, bestiality isn't my thing."

"When are you going to stop fighting me, Judas? We're the same, you and I." She paused. "Well, not the same. I'm higher on the food chain, and you would of course answer to my every whim. But we are of the same mind."

Judas grunted.

Lucy's finger-snakes hissed. One bit into his thigh. He choked back a scream.

"Plague has gone underground. No one can find him. One of my little birds seems to think you're responsible for this."

Fangs dug deeper into the soft part of his thigh. Judas could swear one of them grazed the bone.

"Don't worry, darling. Their venom is drained. I milk them."

"That's something I'd like to see," he said through gritted teeth.

"I'll arrange it."

Sweat broke out on Judas's brow. Daring further rebuke, he grabbed the snake that'd embedded itself in his leg and yanked upward. The pain was petrifying. Twin splotches of blood spread across his pants.

Lucy snarled. "You can't win. You're a decomposing traitor with nothing to your name other than a few words. Plague was a piece of shit. Anyone can mold shit. Famine and Disease will devastate these *people*," she spat the word, "like nothing you've ever seen."

"We'll see."

She laughed. "Oh, Judas. Dear, naive, disgusting Judas. I want to be there when you try to talk your way around Death. What a show that will be."

"I'll send for hors d'oeuvres." He clutched his leg. God, it hurt.

"No need." She ran her forked tongue over his lips. "I'll eat you."

"Aren't you above false threats, Lucy?"

Growling, she thrust her hand, snakes now claws, into his mouth. A sharp pop rang in the back of his head, and his mouth filled with the taste of copper.

Lucy displayed her prize: a molar, yellow with age. She placed it delicately on her tongue. She sucked for a moment and then crunched until she swallowed with an audible gulp.

"Appetizer," she said and was gone.

Loose fabric from the roof of the car served as a suitable bandage for Judas's leg. He stuffed a wad of napkin in the hole where his tooth used to be and wished for some wine, but not that prissy stuff they made now. Real wine like he would siphon from his father's stash. Two glasses of that stuff would render even the largest of men incoherent, and incoherence was just what Judas craved.

Lucy was right. He wouldn't be able to manipulate Death the way he'd done Plague. Getting to Famine would even be a stretch. She was ruthless and liked to play games.

But before Judas could even think of going after her, he needed to sleep. The blood moon was high in the sky, visible over the ghostly lights of the empty city.

He tipped the seat back and settled into a slightly more comfortable position, using his jacket as a blanket. Just a few hours of rest. That'd set everything right in his brain. He'd wake up with a better plan for the Horsemen and a way to get Rain away from Francine. It would all be fine.

He closed his eyes and fell into an uneasy sleep.

CHAPTER NINETEEN

THEY TOOK STACY'S CAR. RAIN drove. She needed something solid to focus on, and it was easier to keep her gaze away from Francine, who stared at her from the passenger seat.

The roads were eerily empty. It felt like the end of the world. Tears burned Rain's eyes because she knew that it was.

The windows of her mother's house were dark. Rain tried not to take that as a bad omen. Electricity was used sparingly and only in emergencies in the Johnson house. But still, she expected at least the flicker of a candle being carried through the front room.

Rain shook her head. What need would the Antichrist have of candles, symbols of hope and wisdom?

"I'm not going in there," Ashly said.

Stacy scoffed.

"No one asked you to." Mary punched his leg.

"None of you are." Francine opened her door. "Rain and I will go in. You wait here."

Rain's stomach turned. Even Francine's voice had changed. Where was the pixie jingle of her laugh? The way her tone brightened at the end of every sentence?

"No," Rain said. "I'm going alone. Just in case." She shot a look into the back seat. She'd never be able to forgive herself if anything happened to those three. They'd trusted and followed her blindly. They were her responsibility now.

But could she leave them with Francine? Her scorn cut through the dark like a jagged knife.

There wasn't a choice. Given the alternative... No, they were safer with Francine. Three against one weren't terrible odds.

"Rain," Mary objected.

"I'll be right out." *I hope.*

Rain closed the door quietly behind her and crept up the walk to the front door. She remembered the camera poised above it, so she kept close to some small shrubbery for cover.

Her hand grazed the doorknob just as she heard footsteps behind her. Rain spun and met Mary's face inches from her own. "What the hell are you doing?"

"I'm not letting you go in there alone."

Rain should have sent her back to the car, but she was grateful not to have to cross the threshold alone.

Rain nodded. "Fine. Stay close to me, and if I tell you to run, you do it. Deal?"

"Deal."

Inside, the dark was all-consuming. Rain felt Mary grab her hand. "It stinks in here."

"Incense." Among other things. Beneath the sharp scents of eucalyptus and jasmine was something earthier, like freshly churned compost and something else barely detectable below that, an animal scent. Wet dog. Human shit.

To anyone else, it would probably have felt as though the house had been abandoned a long time ago. Rain knew better. The incense was fresh. A few hours old, maybe. While strong when it first burned, it didn't linger in the air.

Rain pulled Mary close enough to feel her breath. It was a terrible idea to come here without back up. Jude would have told her that. Judas. For the second time in as many hours, she felt a twitch in that lizard part of her brain that made her question the decision to send him away.

Too late to turn back. The devils were inside the walls and no doubt watched her with glowing, hungry eyes.

She felt along the walls for a light switch. The first she touched had been ripped from the wall and dangled by a single wire.

"Wait!" Mary snatched her hand from Rain's grip.

"What? What's wrong?"

Click. A tiny flame illuminated Mary's smiling face. "I have a lighter."

They couldn't see farther than a foot or two in front of them, but it was better than nothing. After a brief scavenge of the kitchen, Rain found a pair of candle stumps.

Candles lit, Mary said, "Now we can split up."

"No way."

"We'll cover more ground and get out of here faster. I don't know about you, but I don't want to spend more than five minutes in this creep fest."

Rain gripped Mary's wrist. "Do you not watch horror films? That's how someone ends up with her face sliced off."

Cringing, Mary nodded. "Good point."

Still holding Mary's wrist, Rain pulled her in the direction of the main hallway to the three bedrooms. Images of River's broken, bloody body lying on her too-small bed tormented Rain as she reached the first door. The deadbolt was cracked and barely hanging by a thin rod.

Rain paused. Mary pushed the door open.

No River, thank God, but the damage was unreal. Scorch marks covered the walls, making the room almost unrecognizable. Two twin-sized beds, their mattresses gray and little more than ash, came together in the corner.

Mary gagged, pointing at the headless rocking horse. "I couldn't handle it if we found dead kids here."

"Kids haven't lived here in a long time."

"Smells like burnt hair." Mary plugged her nose. "I'll wait in the hallway. It's getting to me."

Rain nodded, inching toward the beds. Draped over the aluminum headboard of what she knew to be River's bed was a collection of black hair. Teeth clenched, Rain took a few strands between her fingertips. Long, black, and singed at the ends. A slight curl at the other end where it used to rest on her sister's shoulders.

No. Rain refused to believe what her gut was saying. River was not dead. Rain was not too late.

She went out in the hallway. "Mary?"

No answer. Rain poked her head in the bathroom. Empty.

"Mary?" She called a little louder.

"This way." Mary's voice carried from somewhere on the other side of the house.

But Rain didn't find her in the kitchen or the living room. Rain held her breath and walked toward the basement.

The maroon sheet that served as a makeshift door hung defiantly among the wreckage of the living room. The couch had been turned over, cushions shredded, the wood skeleton exposed. The walls were scarred with deep, short gouges in lines of eight. Behind the couch lay a steel hoe, cracked at the center of the handle.

She pulled the sheet aside and took the first step down. Something slick squished beneath her shoe. She fought the urge to scream.

With each step, Rain's heart hammered harder against her ribs. She listened for the sound of steps or breathing. Mary's frantic footsteps seemed miles away.

At the bottom of the stairwell, she froze. Streaks of blood led from beneath her feet to the far corner where her mother's surveillance monitors hung, all dead except for one. It showed Rain, her body rigid, her face white and eyes wide. She didn't bother to look for the camera.

On shaky legs, she followed the trail of blood. If it'd all come from one person, there was little chance that person was still alive.

Three steps. Four steps. Five steps. The candle flame darted under Rain's frantic breath. Six steps. A pair of pale feet with dirty soles and chipped toenails. A scar along the edge of his foot from an accident with a forklift.

Please, no.

Her father sat against the wall, splay-legged and propped up by the metal pole driven through his chest and into the concrete. His head lolled forward.

A sob bloated in Rain's chest. Her knees buckled, and she fell next to her father. The candle rolled into the pool of blood and extinguished.

Someone screamed.

Instant blackness in her mind then sudden awareness. One minute, she was alone; the next, Mary kneeled beside her, clutching Rain's shivering body.

She couldn't stop looking at her father. She wanted to believe that if she stared hard enough, wanted hard enough, begged hard enough, he would wake up. The relief that River could still be alive somewhere did nothing to penetrate the grief.

"Dad," she whispered.

Please.

Please.

Mary stroked her head, but Rain barely felt it.

"I'm sorry," Mary said.

For what? Rain wanted to ask. Any moment now, her father would shake back his head and look up at her with those crinkled, sad eyes and ask what took her so long.

Above them, footsteps and frantic voices.

"The others must have heard you."

Rain gingerly picked up her father's hand. It was cold and dry. She held it between hers to warm it up.

A beam of light fell directly across his body. The darkness had hidden the death in his skin. Now, Rain couldn't ignore it. *Please* was answered with a harsh *No*.

Her father was dead.

"Holy shit," someone murmured.

Rain buried her face in Mary's shoulder and wept.

It felt as though hours passed before she could open her eyes without sobbing. Stacy and Mary helped her to stand. Francine kept to the back, partially hidden by the shadow of the stairwell.

Ashly brushed the beam of the flashlight over the walls like a spotlight. "Guys."

Rain followed Mary's gaze. Painted on the wall directly over her father's head was a message: *The sleeping dragon has awakened. Repent.*

Stacy crossed herself.

"We can't leave him here," Rain said. Evil was a word reserved for fairy tales and dictators, but this house *was* evil, and she would not leave her father to rot in it. Despite a childhood of bullshit, the last thing her father had done for Rain was to help her escape her mother. He'd saved her.

"How?" Ashly gestured to the pole.

Rain swallowed a lump. "Carefully."

"We can do it," Mary said, indicating that Rain should turn away or leave the room.

Rain shook her head. "I'll hold him. You guys get that thing out."

Mary, Stacy, and Ashly gripped the pole. Rain placed one arm around her father's shoulders and the other over his chest. Francine stood over them, aiming Ashly's flashlight directly at the wound.

The Disciples tugged once.

"Jesus, it's really in there," Ashly said, then, shamefully, "Sorry."

"On the count of three," Mary ordered. "One... two... three."

Grunting, they managed to pull the pole from the wall, jostling her father's body forward as it slid through him. His head lolled back.

Rain choked.

Her father's eyes were gone. In their place, she saw gaping holes with dried blood crusting the edges.

Francine crouched next to Rain. Her lips brushed her ear. "The eyes are windows to the soul," she whispered.

They wrapped her father's body in a sheet Mary rescued from one of the bedrooms upstairs. It had once been a deep blue with childish pastel stars but had since faded, and the colors bled into each other. Rain didn't recognize it.

She refused to just stuff her father in the trunk of the car, so Mary, Rain, and Stacy all sat in the back, holding him in their laps. Ashly drove, claiming car sickness, and Francine resumed her stoic post in the passenger seat. Every once in a while, Rain caught her staring at them in the vanity mirror. She'd had no kind words or gestures of comfort for Rain. She wore, instead, what looked like grim satisfaction.

Rain cradled her father's head and stroked the strands of hair that had escaped the shroud. Stacy placed a hand on his forehead and mouthed a prayer.

Rain wanted to tell her it was too late. If Francine's last statement could be trusted—and why couldn't it? She'd said it with so much, for lack of a better word, *gusto*—then her father's soul, if there was such a thing, was gone. He was a husk.

Rain leaned her head back against the seat, and tears streaked her checks.

"Almost there," Ashly said.

Stacy had offered a space in her church's cemetery. Her father wouldn't have a gravestone, but he would have a resting place in sacred ground, and that, Stacy said, was the important thing.

With a pair of shovels retrieved from a garden shed at the back of the church, Mary and Rain dug a shallow grave. By the end of it, mud streaked their clothes and face. The physical exertion and repetitive motion—stab, lift, toss, stab, lift, toss—helped to clear the fog in Rain's head. She held out little hope that River was still alive, but she needed to find her, too.

Rain helped Mary climb out of the grave. Mary and Ashly went inside the church to look for some kind of protective covering for her father's body. Stacy stayed, anointing him and praying.

Rain leaned against the planted shovel for support. Now that the digging was over, a creeping weakness set in. A shadow fell over her, and she looked up. Francine stood at the head of the grave, arms at her sides. The way the moon's red glow surrounded her body, her sharp features and shape perfectly proportioned, Rain fully believed that Francine had been an angel. If ever there was a poster child for intelligent design, she was it. On the outside, she was beautiful.

"The dragon is awake," Francine said.

Obviously, Francine wasn't even going to try to fake it.

Fine. Rain wouldn't, either. "So I heard."

"You know what you have to do, don't you?"

"Yes. I have to bury my dad."

"Do you plan to bury them all?"

"Is that a threat?"

Francine tipped her head.

"Whatever you're trying to say, just spit it out."

Francine circled the grave like a bobcat. "The End of Days is here. You know this. There is no avoiding death. Even for you. *Especially* for you. The Dragon not only kills the body, it devours the soul. Humanity will not only die, it will cease to exist. The Eternal Kingdom will close its gates to all."

"Unless?"

"Unless you fight her."

"Find me Excalibur, and I'll get right on it." The grave was deep enough, but Rain began to dig further anyway. She needed something to do with her hands to keep them from shaking.

"You have to fight... and lose. When the Dragon devours the soul of the most innocent, of the Messiah, the souls of humanity will be saved."

"And I suppose this stops the end of the world, too?" Rain's voice shook.

"No. This world will end, but we'll all be called home."

"And if I refuse?"

"I'll just have to persuade you."

"And how do you intend to do that?"

Silence.

Rain glanced up. Francine was gone, replaced with an almost tangible absence of life. Rain couldn't hear Stacy's murmur. Mary and Ashly should have been back by now.

Panic seized her.

Gripping roots and using the shovel for leverage, Rain scrambled out of the grave. Her father's body hadn't been moved, but Stacy was nowhere in sight. Neither was Francine.

Rain ran for the church. The heavy, cathedral-style front doors were thrown open.

Inside, the candelabras on either side of the altar illuminated the bodies of the Disciples, piled in a broken heap at the feet of a statue of an angel, its wings wide, arm thrusting a spear into the air.

Their eyes were gone.

Mary's mouth dangled open as if she were screaming. Along her arms, scrawled in blood, Rain read, *Fight me.*

A torrent of anger and grief wracked Rain's body. She swayed on her knees, fighting to keep conscious. Lips moist with tears, she kissed their foreheads.

I'm so sorry.

And then.

I'll kill her.

Both of them.

It took all night, but Rain dug three more graves near her father's. Exhausted, running on the fumes of the fire burning in her veins, she laid their bodies to rest and spoke over them the only prayer she knew.

"Now I lay me down to sleep..."

CHAPTER TWENTY

T HE SUNRISE LOOKED WRONG. THE reds were too red. The yellows, too dim, like a light bulb on the verge of burning out. Judas watched in awe.

Where the hell are You? You could stop this.

Mysterious ways, a faint voice said.

Always had to have the last word, didn't He? *Fuck Your mysterious ways.*

Judas moved the car into a lot where it was less likely to get towed. Not that there were police around. A few people had ventured out, the looks on their faces a mix of suspicion and fear, fear of the end of the world, but barring that, fear of losing their jobs.

"You're all sheep!" Judas yelled as he struggled to extract his sore body from the car.

No one noticed.

His leg hurt. Dried blood adhered his pants to his thigh, and with each movement, hair and several layers of skin tore from his leg. The off-the-cuff dentistry seemed to do its job, leaving Judas with a sore jaw but without a mouthful of blood and shorn gums. If he could keep from tonguing the hole, it might heal, or at least wouldn't get worse. The expiration date of his body was still unclear. The burn on his face, courtesy of Lucy, still looked as bad as the day it'd happened. Maybe it was just her.

With no other idea where to start, Judas set out on foot to check out what restaurants, coffee shops, anywhere that served food, were open. Famine liked to fuck with people, so the rumor went. Exhibit A: Last night's ruined hotdog. She wouldn't be working on a grand scale like Plague. She'd get personal, like the demons.

There was no way the water epidemic had been solved overnight. Judas didn't hold out much hope that shopkeepers and patrons would just ignore the faint smell of blood in the air. Still, out of some blind masochism others might call faith, he searched. Reward finally showed itself after a few blocks. A blue and red "Open" sign illuminated the window of a cafe called the Greasy Nut. A handwritten sign next to it read: *I assure you we are open. Fresh coffee. Bottled water. Everything half price.*

The air inside was thick with syrup and bacon grease. Booths with cracked plastic cushions lined the walls. The avocado-colored linoleum came up in so many places it was a wonder the ancient waitress didn't trip as she puttered between the occupied tables.

"Sit anywhere," she called, laying a plate of pancakes and a trough of syrup in front of a man who could only be described as planetary.

Distracted by pain and stress, Judas almost didn't notice the twins.

Short and blonde with thin, curve-less bodies bordering on emaciation, identical in every physical way except for their makeup, both wore short, denim skirts and tank tops, but the color of their lipstick differed: one a childish pink, the other acid green. They hovered near the table of the planetary man, licking their lips and twirling dry strands of hair.

Judas strode past them and slid into the adjacent booth. Acid Green Lipstick glanced in his direction but quickly returned her attention to the man in front of her.

"You don't want to eat that," Pink Lipstick said, her voice high-pitched and grating. "Look at you, you fat fuck. Disgusting."

The man stared at his plate, drawing designs in the pools of syrup. He didn't seem to hear the girl, but her words found their way into his mind anyway. On his face was an epic battle between hunger and self-loathing. His mouth twisted in a grimace, but desire lit up his eyes.

He cut a slice out of a pancake, stabbed it with his fork, and held it an inch from his mouth, considering it.

"You don't want to," Pink Lipstick said.

Yes I do, he seemed to say and stuffed it between his lips. He chewed viciously, as if he would change his mind if he didn't swallow immediately.

The girls sighed. Pink Lipstick stuck her tongue out at the man.

Green Lipstick cackled. "You're losing your touch."

"Fuck off."

"What do you think? Heart disease?"

"You have no imagination."

Green Lipstick shrugged. "It works."

"It takes forever." Pink Lipstick paused. "Food poisoning."

"Nasty business."

"And? That's what we're here for, isn't it?"

"Point taken. I just don't want to be around when he starts exploding from both ends."

"Didn't need the visual."

"It was your suggestion!"

"Just shut up and do it. We have a lot of ground to cover."

Dread twisted Judas's stomach. Famine and Disease were working together. They were like teenagers. Each on her own was bad enough. Now they had a partner to egg them on. Worst of all, they would never listen to reason.

I'm fucked.

Green Lipstick—Disease—licked her fingertips then jabbed them into his rolling gut. A gurgling noise erupted, and the man gagged.

"Let's get out of here," Famine said.

Judas slipped out the door just as the man touched by Disease vomited.

Outside, Famine and Disease walked with linked arms. Occasionally, they glanced over their shoulders at Judas ambling behind then giggled into each other's ghastly faces.

The sidewalks didn't stay empty for long. Downtown's work force had come from their hidey-holes, carrying bulging backpacks and briefcases. The slosh of thousands of bottles of water was enough to make Judas seasick.

Following the girls was only part of the quickly disassembling plan in his mind. Judas couldn't talk them out of their tasks, but he could distract them. And if he could distract them long enough, then maybe a new, better plan would manifest before things got too sticky. With someone like Disease involved, it would get sticky sooner rather than later.

"Eww. I think some perv is following us, D." Famine stuck her tongue out at Judas.

"Maybe he likes your ass." Disease grabbed Famine's left ass cheek as though to jiggle the flattened skin.

Judas snorted. "Not even if my dick was on fire and your cunts held the last drops of water, girls."

An older woman in a pencil skirt and heels glared.

"Not you," he said and hurried to keep up with the Horsemen—er—girls. They'd quickened their pace, and the distance between them was too wide.

"Your loss." Disease turned toward him, walking backwards, and pinched her nipples. Brown liquid spurted, dripping like shit-colored tears down her white shirt.

"How is that even remotely attractive?"

The girls shrugged.

"I guess after having your cock in one of those harp-toting cretins, it's hard to approach a real female," Famine said.

"Fuck off."

Disease shushed her.

Francine. Would he ever be able to wipe that mistake from his past?

"As much as we'd love to continue with this little talk, we have things to do," Disease said.

"And we're sick of looking at you," Famine added.

Judas couldn't let them out of his sight. "Oh, come on, just when we were getting to know each other?"

Famine frowned. "Don't be a clinger, Judas. It's pathetic."

The girls waved. Disease blew a kiss. A man who happened to be walking in stride with her caught the tail end of her breath and collapsed.

"Whoopsie," Disease said.

The girls turned and ran.

Judas charged after them, shoving through the crowd that gathered around the collapsed man. As he stepped over the body, he noticed the man's lips were blue.

As they ran, Disease tapped the shoulders of people crossing Judas's path, creating a row of convulsing bodies he struggled to jump over. The wound in his thigh began to bleed again. He felt the trickle collect in his shoe.

Once they noticed the rate at which bodies dropped, the crowd rushed into the street.

A cab turned the corner fast and mowed down a shrieking woman.

The bodies on the sidewalk foamed at the mouth.

"Get out of the way!" Judas yelled, pushing people into the grass as he ran.

The girls picked up speed, their giggles riding the wave of panicked cries of the people struggling to escape what looked like an outbreak of some deadly virus.

Judas gritted his teeth against the pain in his thigh.

They disappeared around the corner of a brick building, and Judas prayed they'd hit a dead end.

It was an alley with a dumpster near the opening, blocked at the end by a twenty-foot cement wall. It would be impossible for him to scale, but that didn't mean the girls couldn't have made it over. Judas struggled to catch his breath while he ran his hands along the wall, looking for foot holes or a clue as to how they managed to leap over it so quickly.

Nothing.

He turned to the dumpster. If it was empty, he could maybe push it against the wall and climb over that way.

Judas limped to it and then lifted the lid. He was met with a pair of bulging, orange eyes. Before he had to time to react, a hot, callused hand gripped his neck and yanked him inside.

CHAPTER TWENTY-ONE

RAIN DREAMED OF FIRE. A kaleidoscope of flames surrounded her naked body, lashing at her skin like whips. Her arms and legs tingled as the pain turned to numbness. She cried out. Then there was laughter. A kiss. And finally, mercifully, a diaphanous creature smothered the fire with a cloak.

She woke with pain in her head and back but couldn't feel her extremities. It was cold. Someone had covered her with a jacket, probably saving her from pneumonia. Wafts of perfume and cake drifted from the collar as Rain sat up.

The shovel lay next to her, stained with a mixture of mud and blood. Her hands were stiff. Blisters pocked her palms and stung when she wiggled her fingers.

Tears burned her eyes, but she blinked them back. She couldn't afford to waste her time on tears.

As Rain stood and made a futile attempt to brush the crusted mud off her arms and face, a figure approached from the church. Tall, bald, he wore a red and black flannel shirt and construction worker boots. Rain wondered how long he'd been there, if he'd seen her burying the disciples, if she should run.

He held his hand out long before he was close enough to shake her hand. Cavernous lines creased his forehead, and his eyebrows were like white spiders. When Rain didn't accept his hand, he smiled and crossed his arms.

"I'm impressed."

She raised her eyebrow.

He nodded to the four haphazard mounds behind her. "Work like that woulda taken me a coupla days."

Fuck. He *had* seen her. The last thing she needed was some nosy bastard—

"Listen," the man said, taking a step forward, "Don't worry, okay? I know…" He paused. "I'm not going to get in your way."

Rain leaned back, poised to either run or swing with both fists. "I don't know what you're talking about."

He chuckled. "They said you were feisty."

"They who?"

"Good guys. Told me to keep an eye on you out here."

"So you've been spying on me."

"Kind of in the job description." He made circles with his fingers and held them over his eyes like glasses and grinned.

"Watcher?"

He nodded.

"Like Francine?"

He nodded again then shook his head. "No, no. Well, yes, but no. She's a little crooked."

Rain's face warmed. "Politicians are crooked. Francine is an evil twat."

"Can't argue with you."

Mentioning Francine ignited new energy in Rain. Standing there talking wasn't going to get her any closer to finding her sister and the dragon. She tossed the jacket to the man. "Listen…"

"Gregory."

"Gregory. I've got things to do. What do you want?"

The harshness in her tone didn't seem to affect him. "Me? Nothing. Just passing on a message."

"Well, go on, then."

"I was told to tell you to go home."

Rain snorted. "Fuck that."

Gregory shrugged. "I'm just the messenger. But if you'll excuse my saying so, you look like you could use a shower. Maybe a Band-Aid.

No reason to make it easier on them by walking into a fight already beat up."

"I'm fine."

"Suit yourself, kiddo." He bent over and picked up the shovel. "You run along. I'll finish things up here."

Rain glanced at the nearest mound. She'd fashioned a cross out of twigs and a strip of cloth to stand sentry over her father's grave.

"Go home," Gregory said. "Trust me."

"I don't trust you."

"Probably the smart thing at this point. Still."

Rain considered him. There was something he wasn't telling her. There was always something they weren't telling her. "What's at home?"

Gregory chuckled, touched his nose, then turned to the first mound and began smoothing the surface with the back of the shovel in wide, graceful motions.

Why could she never get a straight answer out of any of these people? *Fine, home it is.*

The grip on Judas's throat loosened only after he'd been slammed into a chair and his arms and legs tied. The heat was stifling. Each breath in burned at the back of his throat and hung heavy in his lungs.

Judas's captor stood in front of him, a crazed grin on his face. Calloused skin, scorched in places, covered his face. His eyes were like two chunks of smoldering coal.

Famine and Disease giggled somewhere inside the room, their laughter echoing about the stone walls.

Judas struggled against his bonds. "Okay, okay, you've had your little laugh. Now let me out of here."

Francine emerged from the shadows wearing a too-smug grin. "I'm afraid that's not going to happen."

Her presence hit him like a punch to the gut. He wasn't surprised to see her in league with the likes of the idiot twins. But if she was here, that meant Rain had been put on the path Francine wanted her on and walked purposefully toward her doom. She was as good as dead.

"What've you done with Rain?"

Francine shrugged. "I gave her a nudge."

One of the Bobbsey Twins from Hell cleared her throat. "Excuse me, but I thought you said we'd get to have fun, not listen to you two talk about your pet."

Judas tugged on the thick ropes that cut into his fingers. "If I'd have known this was going to be a party, I would've brought booze."

Francine grinned. "Don't waste your strength. Those ropes were forged in the very fires of Hell. Your half-dead limbs would fall off before they made it through. We wouldn't want that."

"We wouldn't?" Disease stepped forward, pouting.

Francine shot her a look that could've pierced armor. "Not yet."

"Fun, first?"

"Yes, child. Fun, first." Francine turned and approached a tall white armoire with scorch marks up the sides.

"Not really in the mood for fun, thanks. Fast approaching apocalypse and all that." Speaking winded Judas. Breathing had become a chore.

The doors of the armoire opened wide. Small slices of light in the room glinted off the many metal tools and contraptions hanging there. Francine clasped her hands and sighed. "Aren't they lovely, Judas?"

He seethed.

She selected a small dagger from the center of the collection and turned to face him. "You tried to get in the way. I got you out of that piss hole of a room, and this is the thanks you gave me. What an ungrateful wretch you are."

"I'll take ungrateful wretch over deluded half-angel any day."

"Would you, now?" Francine grinned, slashing his chin with the blade.

He felt the blood trickle down his neck. The wound burned as the putrid air caressed it like a diseased tongue. Judas clenched his jaw against the pain. Francine wouldn't leave until she'd gotten a rise out of him. She was too proud, too pompous. He hoped he could use it to his advantage. If Francine was here, hurting him, then she couldn't be near Rain, prodding her like a heifer on her way to slaughter.

Judas sat up straighter. "I would. Tell me, Francine. How does it feel to be cast aside like a snotty tissue?"

"I will take back what is rightfully mine."

"And what would that be, pumpkin?"

Francine sneered, bringing the dagger close enough to his mouth for his breath to fog the blade. "Home, Judas." She spat his name. "Once this is over, I will return to Trinity's halls. I will be rewarded for showing Him the error of His ways."

"Error?"

"Don't play stupid with me. We only did as He had done. We loved and protected his most beloved creation. Unlike some"—she cast a glance over her shoulder at the stoic creature guarding the door—"we harbored no resentment. How fair was it, then, that we were thrown away? That I was told I was not worthy of his *mercy*?"

"Don't be an idiot."

Francine cracked the side of Judas's head with the hilt of the dagger. Bolts of pain shot through his body. The room spun, making his stomach lurch.

"You're the idiot if you think you can stop me with a little gab fest. Do you know what I think?"

He swallowed against the rising bile in his throat. "Pray, tell."

"I think you'll give up. You think you're being brave, tied to this chair while your blood drips into your lap. I know you, Judas. Once the girls get their hands on you, you'll crumble. And do you know why? Because in the end, the only thing that matters to you is your own skin. Oh, and these." Francine pulled a velvet bag from her pocket and emptied its contents on the dirt floor in front of him. Silver coins.

Judas shook his head. "You're wrong."

"Am I? Let's see, shall we?"

She spun the dagger in her hand before sliding it into her belt. A wink in his direction, and then she nodded at the girls in the corner. Judas could almost smell their giddiness. They would take their time. Enjoy themselves. The only question that remained was how long he would be able to take it.

"You're using Rain just like He used you," Judas said.

Francine licked her lips. "Eye for an eye," she said and strode from the room.

Disease and Famine didn't take long to choose their tools: Disease, a long, curved blade like one meant for gutting animals, Famine, a black leather glove covered in tiny spikes.

"Bad boy." Famine slapped his face.

Blood filled Judas's mouth. He spat and braced himself for seconds.

CHAPTER TWENTY-TWO

THE AIR IN THE APARTMENT was stale and smelled of week-old garbage. Rain left the door open to thin the stench. Not knowing what to expect inside, she examined her surroundings from the doorway. Other than a pair of underwear on the kitchen floor she couldn't remember leaving, the apartment seemed to be exactly as she'd left it.

"Okay," Rain muttered, making her way slowly down the hallway.

The door to Francine's room was closed. That in and of itself wasn't unusual, but Rain realized that she hadn't been in the girl's room in weeks. Months. There'd never been the chance. Every time she'd turned around, there Francine was, all smiles and insistence and sex.

Rain shuddered. Had sleeping with Francine *done* anything to her? Was she marked somehow?

Pushing the thought aside, she gripped the doorknob and turned.

Cold crushed the breath from Rain's lungs. She coughed hard and wrapped her arms over her chest. Shivers wracked her legs and shoulders. Rain's eyes struggled to adjust to the darkness, despite the little sunlight shining through the blinds. Francine's bed sat nestled in the corner, blanket creaseless and pillows without a dent. It was as though it'd never been slept in. Francine's sculptures were nowhere to be found, and what little furniture Rain remembered being there—a small, white dresser and a sloppily painted table—were missing.

Not only was Francine gone from Rain's life, it was as though she'd never even been there. Rain felt no grief over the loss. Only cold.

She turned to leave and caught a glimpse of something shiny out of the corner of her eye. Venturing farther into the room, Rain scanned the floor. Barely protruding from beneath the bed, tucked against the leg of the bedframe, was the tip of a blade. Rain dropped to her stomach and wormed up to the bed. Reaching underneath, fingertips numb from the cold, she gripped the hilt of the blade—a sword—and pulled it from its hiding place.

The hilt was hot, as if it'd been sitting on black asphalt beneath a mid-July sun for hours, and embedded in the blade were flecks of what looked like rubies. The hilt itself appeared to be made of solid gold.

"Whoa," Rain murmured.

She stood and held the sword in front of her. It was as long as her arm but no heavier than a hardback book. Rain swung it easily, enjoying the *whoosh* of it slicing through the air.

"Like it?" a female voice said behind her.

Rain stumbled, bringing the blade down onto the bed. It sliced cleanly through the mattress, stopped only by the metal bedframe.

She turned.

Lily stood in the doorway. "It looks like you could use some practice."

Rain grimaced. "Yeah."

The ground shuddered. A sound like thunder shook the walls.

"Unfortunately, there's not time for that. As we speak, Lucifer is assembling her hordes for ascension."

"With Francine."

Lily nodded sadly. "Yes. She's lost. I tried to convince her..."

"There was nothing you could do. She's a bitch with an agenda. No amount of reasoning can sway such a beast. Trust me. I know."

Lily blushed.

"Stupid question: why was this in here?" She held up the sword.

"You loved Francine. We needed you to see that the woman as you knew her wasn't real, that her heart was as empty as this room."

Rain sighed. "So what exactly do I have to do?"

"It's simple, really. Kill the dragon."

"You mean my mother." Rain's voice faltered at the mention of the woman. Her father's crumpled body flashed in her mind, and her eyes burned with new tears.

Lily placed a delicate hand on her shoulder. "It's the only way. I'm sorry."

Rain gripped the hilt, feeling the weight of it. A mixture of anxiety and adrenaline pulsed through her body and seemed to enter the sword itself. It was almost as though it vibrated against her palm with its power and her purpose.

She looked Lily directly in the eyes. "I'm not."

Outside, the war had already begun. While the soldiers of the horde remained hidden, the damage they left with their arrival spelled out their intent. Buildings smoldered atop caving foundations. Bodies lay twisted on scorched grass. Black smoke blotted out the sun.

Rain crept along the broken side streets with one hand on the sword threaded through her belt. With each block, the damage grew. They could have chosen anywhere to release the dragon, but she had a feeling she would know where to find it. They *needed* her to.

As Rain neared the center of the city, siren wails drowned out the pounding of her heart. She was getting close.

A growl erupted behind her, raising every hair on her body. She spun around, tripping on a crack in the road, and twisted her ankle. Pain shot up her leg, and she struggled to correct herself.

It's too early for this shit.

Rain pulled the sword from her belt, slitting it in the process, and searched for the source of the sound. A demon with the torso of a human and the lower body of a snake slithered toward her, leaving a trail of black ooze in its path. Its forked tongue flicked the air, tasting the fear that pulsed off her in waves. She held the sword out, gripping it with both hands, trying to ignore the pain in her ankle. There was no way she could outrun it.

Heartbeat pounding behind her eyes, she swallowed hard. "Come on, then, ugly."

The demon hissed, exposing long, pointed teeth. It moved faster than it should have, raising its clawed hands. Rain slashed wildly, missing at first. The second swing connected with the side of its head, cutting through it like butter. Gurgling, the demon collapsed at her feet. Putrid smog erupted from the carcass.

She gagged and fell backward into an alley, knocking her elbows against a dumpster.

Someone screamed, and for a moment, Rain wondered if it was her.

She heard another shout, distant and near and the same time, echoing as if it came from inside a tin can. She turned.

It came from inside the dumpster.

The colors and shapes of the room bled together, spinning in endless circles before Judas's eyes. Disease lashed his neck with a whip for what could have been the tenth or thousandth time. He didn't feel the pain. He saw it bursting in yellows and reds and whites. Fireworks.

Orange. A bright streak of it rushed by, twirling, scattering its rays like the sun. As Judas struggled to focus on its source, he heard guttural cries of pain not unlike his own, but his mouth was closed.

Someone called his name.

He coughed.

"Judas."

The ropes tying him to the chair fell away. Relief flooded his wrists and ankles. He breathed deeply and closed his eyes, allowing them to adjust.

When Judas opened them again, the room was more or less back into focus. Blood pooled around the bodies of Famine, Disease, and their mute guard. Disease still clutched her whip like a lifeline.

He spit on her.

"Are you okay? Can you stand?"

Judas looked up and met Rain's worried gaze. He could have cried for the gratitude he felt. Instead, he nodded and lurched to his feet. "You came."

"What kind of Messiah would I be if I didn't?"

Judas grinned. "The shitty kind."

"Exactly."

"How did you—" He noticed the sword dangling at her side. Beautiful and familiar, it only took a moment for the realization to hit him. "The sword of Gabriel."

"The what?"

"The sword of the Archangel Gabriel. When God sent the angel of death to slaughter the firstborn sons of Egypt, that was the tool he used. I've never seen it up close."

And now that he had, Judas wasn't sure he wanted to. The kind of tool that could be used to kill demons in the hands of someone as small and uncoordinated as Rain was deadly indeed. He sensed the vibrations of destruction radiating from it.

"It was given to me by one of the Grigori."

He flinched. Grigori. Francine. Judas would kill the backstabbing bitch if it was the last thing he did. "We need to get out of here."

Rain started back the direction she came.

"Wait." Judas headed for the cabinet of horrors his captors had used to draw as much anguish from him as they could. He snatched the longest knife from the rack. "Now we can go."

CHAPTER
TWENTY-THREE

*W*E'VE GOT THE BUILDING SURROUNDED. *Come out with your hands up.*

The echo of a megaphone met Rain's ears the moment she emerged from the weird dumpster portal where Judas had been kept. She'd know that voice anywhere. It was Detective Park.

"Poor bastards. They think they've got her cornered," Judas said.

He put on a brave face, but Rain could tell he was in pain. He limped behind her, breathing heavily. His skin was in tatters, and each movement forced crusted wounds open to bleed again. Part of her wanted to tell him to stay away, to go back to his motel, but the other part knew he wouldn't listen.

"Why'd you do it?"

He shrugged. "She was hot and persuasive."

"No, I mean—"

"I know what you mean." He sighed. "Those were complicated times in my life. I'd taken up with a man who claimed to be the Messiah when I should have been taking care of my sister. She had no dowry, our father was dead, and my brothers were useless. When the Romans got involved, they threatened all of us with our lives and the lives of our families to give him up. A man will do terrible things when he's scared."

"Are you scared now?"

Judas looked away.

"Well," Rain said, "with the cops there, I won't get anywhere near her."

"I think they've got more on their minds than arresting a suspected eco-terrorist."

Rain waved her sword. "They might get nervous with this around."

"Oh."

"If I could get around them, maybe. Get inside the building…"

Judas snapped his fingers. "Say no more." He started off in the direction of the barricade, grunting with each step.

"Where are you going?"

He waved his knife. "To cause some trouble."

"They'll shoot you."

Judas shrugged. "Probably."

Judas was out of good ideas. A bad one would have to do. He'd never been shot before, but he imagined it couldn't feel worse than what he'd endured over the last few hours. *Boom, boom. Splat, splat.* Game over. Quick. Easy. He'd welcome it with open arms.

But what of his afterlife?

Best not to think about that now. It might make you change your mind.

Judas slid the knife into the back of his belt and limped toward the barricade.

They didn't notice him until he was practically on top of them. Detective Park spotted him first. He waved. Her eyes widened. God only knew what he looked like. Broken. Beaten. Torn to shreds.

Good, Judas thought.

"Step away, sir," Detective Park shouted. "This is a dangerous area."

"You're telling me. That's why I'm here."

He pulled the knife from his belt and waved it around, slashing the air, pirouetting, like a brain-damaged pirate.

The click of several guns being aimed at him sent a shiver down Judas's spine.

"Drop the knife, sir."

"And ruin my chances of being the hero? Never."

"Sir, I'll give you to the count of three."

Here we go, he thought, and stabbed an invisible foe.

"One."

Deep breath.

"Two."

You'd better be moving, Rain.

There was a grunt in his ear, and the next thing he knew, Judas was facedown on the street, his cheek being scraped against the asphalt.

"Shut up and stay down," the man who tackled him spat.

"You mind laying off the arm? I think it's broken."

The man kept him flat on the ground, but out of the corner of his eye, Judas saw a streak of orange rush into the building.

The foyer of the building smelled of rotten eggs and scorched flesh. Bodies littered the room. Most looked bitten in half. All were eyeless. Above it all, soft violin music played. Rain's mother was here somewhere.

A dark hallway led to an escalator, blocked by a lifeless woman whose jacket was lodged in the bottom. Rain stepped over the body and began a cautious ascent, glancing back over her shoulder with each step. As she climbed, the music grew fainter until the only sounds were Rain's rapid breath and pounding heart.

The second floor was lit by a single, flickering lamp. The rest of the light fixtures were in pieces, crunching beneath her feet. The stench up here was stronger. Rain stifled a gag.

"Dearest Rainfall…"

She turned her head so hard her neck cracked. River sat cross-legged on the floor, eyes thin and yellow, arms limp on her knees. Her once long, lustrous hair was gone, leaving a jagged buzz atop her head. If it weren't for the fire in her eyes, she would have looked meditative.

She tipped her head. "You came."

Rain gripped the hilt of the sword in sweaty, shaking hands. "You're alive."

"Of course I am. Why wouldn't I be?"

The revelation was like a punch to the solar plexus. "Wh-Where's Mom?" Rain stammered.

River chuckled. "Mom. You know, I always found it funny how she unleashed herself on me more often than you. It was almost as if she knew something."

Rain's head spun. Spots flickered in the corners of her vision, and she fought her body's cues to pass out. It couldn't be true. "Mom is dangerous."

"Was dangerous. In her own way, I suppose." River whistled, and a sheet that'd been covering something tall and thin flew to her. Their mother's decapitated head sat on a pike, eyes burned from their sockets.

Rain swallowed a rush of vomit.

"You don't know how long I've waited to do that," River crooned.

The sword felt heavier in Rain's hand. "But Francine said—"

"You believed her? Oh, dear, sweet Rainfall. Cynical as you think you are, your naïveté astounds."

"You killed Dad."

"He was in the way."

"And Mom."

"Even you can admit she deserved it."

Rain swallowed. "My friends?"

Smiling, River nodded. "My best work yet. Subtlety would never have worked on you." She examined her nails. "Although, when I finish with you, well, that'll be my masterpiece."

"You're not my sister." Rain's muscles twitched with new adrenaline. "River would never—"

"There is no River, you sniveling little twit. It was always me."

Tears burned Rain's eyes. "Fuck you."

River stood. "Now, now, Rainfall. You're making me angry."

There is no River. Just this… thing. More people will die if you don't just—Rain clenched her fist around the sword and breathed deeply. *Stop talking, and do it already. Do it.*

Rain lunged at her, sword extended, but River easily sidestepped the effort.

"So be it," she said.

As she growled, River's skin fell away in chunks, revealing an opalescent black under-skin. She grew at a terrifying rate, limbs extending, bending and twisting into sharp talons. Soon, her form took up the length of the room. Rain stumbled backward, catching herself on a shard of glass that dug into her palm. Pain exploded up her arm. River's skull cracked and reformed. She looked like an alligator with side eyes and a jaw that could crush bone.

Rain scrambled on her knees toward the escalator, dragging the sword in her uninjured hand.

River's voice boomed from the mouth of the dragon, "Accept your death, Rainfall."

Tears streaked down Rain's face, blurring her vision. Using the sword as a crutch, she lifted herself up and ran as fast as her legs would move down the escalator, aiming for the door.

Judas fumed, cuffed in the backseat of a cop car. He almost would rather they shoot him than leave him here, where he was forced to watch and worry with no way of doing anything to help. Sure, he'd made it easier for her to get to the dragon. Next was the hard part.

Judas slammed his feet against the seat back. He shouldn't have let her go in alone. What the hell had he been thinking?

Coward, he thought. *Like always.*

At the front of the barricade, cops wearing riot gear marched forward with snipers crouched low behind them. They closed in on the door. It burst open, and Rain ran through, sword dragging, sending sparks up from the concrete. Her arm gushed blood. And her face—nothing could describe the fear etched there.

"Let me out!" he pleaded. "Let me... Oh, God."

The building's door blew out, crumbling much of the front of the building and sending Rain flying forward. The dragon appeared behind the dust. Black ooze streamed from its snout. Its serpent-like body slithered forward. The stupid riot cops fell over themselves trying to get away while snipers aimed at its head. Their bullets wouldn't do any good.

Judas smashed his fists against the glass then his feet. Nothing helped. He screamed for someone, anyone, to unlock the Goddamn door, but no one was listening. The dragon took its time, picking the cops off, one by one. Its great jaws lurched forward and crunched down on the legs of one of the snipers. His gun fell but not before discharging.

The bullet went straight through Judas's window, missing his head by a hair.

Detective Park peered over the top of her vehicle and screamed, "Open fire!"

Bullets rained on top of the dragon, piercing its flesh, but only just. It broadened its chest, accepting them all like gifts. Judas scanned the crowd, but there was no sign of Rain. He prayed that she'd gotten out of the line of fire in time.

He reared back and rammed his feet into the weakened window. Mercifully, it shattered. Driven by new strength, Judas slithered out, gritting his teeth against the glass slicing into his waist. He hit the ground head first, and pain rang through his skull. Every muscle in his body protested as he wrenched himself to standing. Judas was out, but his wrists were still cuffed.

The ground rumbled beneath his feet with the roars of the dragon. Bullets flew. He kept his head low and searched for the cop who'd cuffed him. The poor fuck wasn't far. At least, the top half of him wasn't. Judas's stomach turned as he searched the corpse for a key.

Yes!

With fingers slick with the cop's blood, Judas slid the key into the lock. Turned. Freedom.

He stood, rubbing his wrists just as the firing stopped. Rain emerged from between two cars. Judas had to stop himself from calling out to her. The dragon, mouth full of masticated cop, didn't seem to have noticed her yet.

"Slowly," he urged under his breath. "Don't do anything stupid."

Rain raised the sword over her head and let out a battle cry to rival the warriors from Judas's time. She charged toward the dragon's belly in long, elegant strides.

Judas hadn't the time to react. The dragon spread her body wide, casting a thick shadow over them all, like a scaly cloud. It sucked in a great breath.

Rain was so close.

The dragon exhaled. The torrent of bullets delivered by the police showered from its mouth. Rain's body twitched beneath the avalanche of ammunition pounding into her. Blood sprayed across the asphalt. She fell, and the sword clattered to a halt next to her.

All thought, all physical pain left Judas in an instant.

He ran. His vision tunneled until he saw only Rain. It would be a matter of seconds before the dragon devoured her. As much as Judas might welcome the end of existence, he couldn't, *would not*, let her life end this way.

The sword was almost within reach. If he could just—

A slender leg kicked it away.

Francine.

Judas eyed her shit-eating grin with a fire in his belly and a desperate need to see her body broken and bloody.

"It's over," she said.

Not yet, it isn't. "I'm going to enjoy this." He leapt on top of her.

Angel or not, woman or not, Judas pinned her to the ground, hands around her thin, delicate neck and squeezed. Her eyes bulged but betrayed no sign of fear. He didn't care. He would stare into them, and she would stare back as he slowly crushed the life from…

No.

Judas glanced over his shoulder to see the dragon's face descend upon Rain's body. He looked back at Francine. She smiled.

He relinquished his hold on the twice-fallen angel and scrambled to the sword. Snatching it up, he ran toward Rain.

The dragon opened its mouth. Saliva sizzled as it hit the ground around Rain's body. Judas dove on top of her and felt the pull of the dragon's breath on his very soul. He suddenly felt weak. Too weak. With one final effort, Judas lifted the sword and plunged the blade deep into the dragon's skull.

The effort took the last of him. Everything faded to black.

CHAPTER TWENTY-FOUR

"WAKEY, WAKEY."
Something nudged Judas's shoulder.
"Up and at 'em."

Every atom in every cell of every inch of his body hurt. His fucking eyelashes hurt. If he could have opened his eyes without screaming in agony, he would have.

"Come now, Judas. Someone might think you're milking this."

"Fuck. You." Judas worked his mouth delicately around each syllable.

"I'll forgive that once because I know you've knocked your head."

The voice worked its way through the cotton in his mind until it rang with familiarity. But then that meant...

Judas's forced his eyes open. G stood over him, arms crossed over his chest.

"I'm dead," Judas said.

"Mm."

"Again."

"Went better this time around, don't you think?"

He couldn't tell if G was being sarcastic. It hurt to think about it too hard.

"She died, too," Judas murmured.

"Yes." G tapped a finger on his lips. "And no."

"What do you—"

G shushed him. "I've got another job for you."

Three Days Later

Rain's ear itched.

She knew it was impossible. The last thing she remembered was being blasted with a million bullets from the body of a formerly-her-sister dragon. It'd killed her. And yet, she was very much aware of a tingling sensation all down her left side and a tickle in her ear.

"Don't scratch," a voice said. "You'll fuck up the ointment."

Rain's eyes fluttered open. The light burned like hell. She touched her ear. Her fingers came away slimy.

"I told you not to touch."

Blinking, she turned toward the voice. He wore his irritation openly, frowning at her.

"Judas."

He smiled but quickly shook it off. "You're going to end up with some nasty scars if you don't leave this alone." He smeared a foul-smelling jelly down the left side of her neck.

Rain shook her head. None of it made any sense. Shouldn't she be dead? Wasn't she? As her eyes adjusted to the light, she took in her surroundings: peeling paint on the walls, a single window with safety-cone orange curtains over it, and a matching blanket draped over her. It looked like…

"Are we in your motel room?"

Judas sighed. "Yes. Saved the whole of creation, and He still stuck me in this shithole."

"I don't understand."

He set the jar down and sat on the edge of the bed. "Best not to wonder too much. Your brain will fry."

"It already feels fried."

"Being dead will do that to you."

"I –"

Judas put up his hand. "Just let it go."

Rain struggled to sit up as her frustration mounted. "But what happened?"

He tried to push her back down, but she refused. It felt as though she'd been on her back for days.

"You died. I died trying to stop it. But no matter what I did, it was always meant to happen."

"So why aren't we still dead? Or are we?"

"Being the Messiah affords you certain perks, specifically, a third-day resurrection."

"And you?"

"I'm not. Just here temporarily. Someone had to make sure they didn't bury you."

Rain shuddered at the thought of waking up in a pine box six feet underground. "Thanks."

"Don't thank me. I was all ready to retire to a cloud somewhere, strumming my golden harp and singing my *kyrie elèisons*."

"Bullshit."

He chuckled. "We'll never know, will we?"

Rain wanted to offer a smile in return, but none came. She was alive, but what, really, was the point? Her family was gone. Her supposed lover betrayed her, and if Rain let herself think deeply about it, she knew that Francine had been the orchestrator of it all. People had died because of Rain. Why did she deserve to live?

"Why?" she said, unable to articulate anything else.

"I could give you some bullshit answer about self-sacrifice, but no matter how true it may be, it wouldn't satisfy you. Over and over you'll wonder, why me? Trust me. I've sat in this room thinking about it, and the only real answer I can come up with is *because*."

Rain considered it and then nodded. He was right. "Now what?"

"Now you live. You do what I said to do in the beginning. Show people what it means to be human."

She smacked her dry lips. "Could I have some water first?"

Judas retrieved a glass from the table and filled it with water from the bathroom sink. Rain took the glass and drank greedily. It wasn't until the second gulp that she noticed.

"This is wine."

He snorted. "Like I said. Perks."

193

Judas waited until Rain was asleep before slipping out. She was a smart kid. She'd figure things out on her own.

As promised, G waited in the parking lot for him. G leaned against a hot little red car that looked as though it cost more than the gross national product of a small country.

"Nice."

G shrugged. "I don't normally grant the petty, materialistic prayers, but I was bored."

Judas raised an eyebrow.

"That was good, what you said in there. The *because* crap."

"It's true, isn't it? That's how you work." He pointed to the car. "Doing things out of boredom."

G sighed. "No, Judas. It was because of you."

"Thanks. I wasn't harboring enough guilt as it was."

"Redemption, Judas. Yours. That's what all this was about. Do you really think an idiot like Lucifer and her little twit in training, Francine, could pull one over on me? No. This was all to show you that you could be more. And you did it." He smiled.

"Yeah. Well. Don't look so smug about it."

G patted his shoulder. "You're welcome."

Judas grunted.

"Now what was this I heard about harps and devotionals? You know, I've never heard you sing. I bet your voice is simply *heavenly*."

Acknowledgements

I've HAD A LOT OF people flit in and out of this batshit ride I'll call a writing career, but none have been more ruthless readers, insufferable cheerleaders, and foul-mouthed friends than fellow wordsmiths Renee Miller and Hanna Elizabeth. If one should need an idea (or a severe whipping), one need only visit their cave at the edge of oblivion.

And Crystal. As if you didn't know.

About the Author

Katrina Monroe is a novelist, mom, and snark-slinger extraordinaire.

Her worst habits include: eating pretty much anything with her fingers, yelling at inappropriate times, and being unable to focus on important things like dinner and putting on pants.

She collects quotes like most people collect, well, other things. Her favorite is, "If you have any young friends who aspire to become writers, the second greatest favor you can do them is to present them with copies of The Elements of Style. The first greatest, of course, is to shoot them now, while they're happy." – Dorothy Parker

Readers can revel in her sarcasm at authorkatrinamonroe.wordpress.com or follow her on Twitter, @authorkatm.